Talking in the Dark

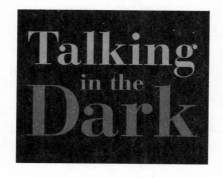

Talking in the Dark

STORIES

Laura Glen Louis

HARCOURT, INC.

New York   San Diego   London

From *Straw for the Fire: From the Notebooks of Theodore Roethke, 1943–63*
arranged by David Wagener, copyright 1972 by Beatrice Roethke.
Published by Doubleday, a division of Random House.

NIGHT AND DAY by Cole Porter
© 1932 (Renewed) Warner Bros. Inc.
All Rights Reserved   Used by Permission
WARNER BROS. PUBLICATIONS U.S. INC. Miami, FL 33014

Crystal Ship and *Light My Fire* by Jim Morrison, John Densmore, Robby
Kreiger, Ray Manzarek, published by Doors Music Company.

Grateful acknowledgment is made to the following
publications in which these stories first appeared:
"Fur," originally published in *Ploughshares,*
was reprinted in *The Best American Short Stories 1994;*
"Her Slow and Steady" appeared in *American Short Fiction.*

www.harcourt.com

Library of Congress Cataloging-in-Publication Data
Louis, Laura Glen.
Talking in the dark: stories/Laura Glen Louis—1st ed.
p. cm.
Contents: Tea—Fur—Her slow and steady—Thirty yards—Rudy's
two wives—Talking in the dark—The quiet at the bottom
of the pool—Divining the waters.
ISBN 0-15-100522-2
I. Title
PS3562.O823 T3   2001
813'.6—dc21   00-046144

Text set in Meridien Medium
Designed by Kaelin Chappell
Printed in the United States of America
First edition
A C E G I K J H F D B

In Memory
Lee Wai Chung
and Bing Wah Louis

Love: looks and sounds like murder.

—Theodore Roethke

Like the beat, beat, beat, of the tom-tom,
When the jungle shadows fall,
Like the tick, tick, tock of the stately clock,
As it stands agaisnt the wall,
Like the drip, drip, drip, of the raindrops,
When the summer show'r is through;
So a voice within me
keeps repeating,
You,
You,
You.

—Cole Porter

CONTENTS

In appreciation of their many gifts and unstinting
efforts, I thank these fine readers:
Jan Wurm, Martha Cook, Ellen L. Wong,
and Thomas Farber. For their staunch support,
guidance, and enthusiasm, I am indebted to
Elyse Cheney and to Walter Bode.

As ever, my profound thanks to Norman and
to Nathan—my port and compass.

Tea

Wu drew a finger along her spine, a cue that she needed to stand taller in the one-legged pose called tree. *Vṛkṣāsana.* Wu drew his finger on up her neck and said, "Ten minutes." That's all he asked of his students: ten minutes. "In the time it takes to boil water for tea," he said, "you could do your daily practice." With her free leg bent, Sheila grounded her standing foot and stretched her leg, her torso, her neck, her arms up, up, up. She struggled for stillness, which even as she was doing it she knew to be oxymoronic. Wu continued around the room, a hundred and fifty-five pounds of bald attention. He led them through a silent string of standing poses that they could do against the base of the kitchen counter while waiting for this ten-minute tea to boil, to steep. *Trikoṇāsana. Vīrabhadrāsana. Adho Mukha Śvānāsana.* Triangle. Warrior. Downward-facing dog. To rest in between they did *Uttānāsana,* a straight-legged, palms-on-the-floor forward bend from the waist, which kids called rag doll, and which Chapman called fuck me.

The water boiled. Sheila reached for the kettle. Wet hair skimmed bare shoulders. Chapman licked a drop of water from her blond curls. Holding her, he stirred gunpowder tea into her cup. His hands were large and callused, workman's hands. Passing him on the street, who would think: biochemist, researcher, arranger of genes— a man who might any day unlock codes that could save lives? Sometimes she wouldn't see him for days and she wondered whose life was he really trying to save? The tea leaves unfurled. Chapman pressed her pubis against the lip of the counter. He unhooked her bra, slipped one hand under the Lycra, the other under her skirt, dipped his fingers wherever they both wanted, and made her give it all up. The tea steamed from her Russian glass cup. Before it ripened, he was gone.

Once or twice, Sheila did try ten-minute yoga as her tea steeped, but most times she grabbed a shower, straightened the bed, skimmed articles about gene manipulations or stockpiled viruses or the newest photos from the Hubble telescope that once again enlarged the universe, whose limits she couldn't begin to imagine. She collated her production reports (on-line drugs) and stuffed them in her bag.

Over the weeks, she realized Wu was right: much could be accomplished in the time it took to make tea. In the time it took to make tea, the direction of a person's life could change. In the time it took for the kettle to whistle and for her to spoon out the leaves, she could read the mail, including a letter from Providence saying she should come in again to redo her Pap. In the time it took for the water to be infused, she realized that once again, as had been his recent habit, Chapman had given her pleasure but desired little for himself. In the time it took the tea on her desk to darken, she could fire the first person on the single-spaced sheet her boss handed her after citing several quarters of seven-figure losses. Ten A.M. By noon she would have to fire three single mothers. One had an advanced degree in medieval art and an autistic child. Sheila stood, nauseous, and tried to comprehend her falling trajectory from programmer to manager to executioner. The Earl Grey released its fragrance of bergamot oil, the last sweet thing of her day.

She walked long steps to the ladies' room. Someone came out, she slipped in.

The beanies talked across the stalls. The beanies worked in accounting and knew even before she did who would be pink-slipped. By the unnatural breaks in her speech—with phrases abutting their predecessors and breaths interrupting her own next idea—Sheila knew the one talking was Mona. Luce had the bloody rose drilled into her ankle. Mona wouldn't name the lover who visited every Tuesday night, but she divulged every kiss and giggle. Last night her nameless faceless lover banged on her door as she was garnishing the steaks. He unzipped her dress and slapped her playfully when he realized that she was wearing nothing underneath. He spread her and examined her and gave her pleasure in the kitchen and the living room and never entered her, and in this way he could still go home to his wife and convince himself he wasn't having an affair. Luce, in an adjacent stall, had been rubbing herself and now stopped. She needed for Mona to continue. Mona said she thought he was lying, to his wife, to her. She said it didn't matter how many times she's made him come with her hands and her breasts and her imagination, and how many times he's phoned her at her desk and whispered—who whispers in the middle of the day?—he never looked at her when she came. Deep down she knew he was right: they weren't truly lovers. Lovers abandoned themselves to every grace, to every fall from grace.

The two women lapsed into silence and each assumed it was the other who had finally let out a stream as heavy as a horse.

Sheila knew Mona's lover wasn't Chapman. But he could have been.

That night in bed, Sheila sat on top and reached back to brace herself against his bent iron-man knees in the most straight-ahead sex they'd had in a long time, and she saw their rutted lives in a flash. The words just slipped out, before she could think.

"I'm not the one, am I?"

Even as his eyes flicked open, his rhythm increased. He held her feet against his hips, held them more tenderly than he ever had, and against her will she felt herself open and open to him. His eyes teared as he took in every inch of her, knowing this would be the last time he would see her so naked.

"No," he said. "You're not the one."

He didn't shelter her with excuses of his own unworthiness, his immaturity, that *he* wasn't right for *her*. Already her body was closing up but he took it to be a heightening. He came. He could.

Sheila packed her toiletries, her nightgown, her sweats, a few books. Three years, and everything that she kept at his house still fit into a zippered bag. On the way out she dropped her copy of his keys on the dining table, as if vacating a weekend rental. The kettle whistled, an expensive, muted tenor. In the time it took to back out of his driveway, to feed into the first entrance to the freeway, to sit in stop-and-go traffic as cars snaked all the way up to the delta and down past the peninsula, the kettle had boiled dry. By the time Chapman returned from Dixie's Two A.M. Club, the bottom of the kettle was glowing red. It gave off a heat and a smell.

Because Chapman was the man she thought she would grow old with—the man who made her laugh, at him, at herself, the man who looked at her sometimes and was stunned speechless, who looked at her as if he

wanted to fill and fill her with child, and then name
them both as beneficiaries of all his love, the man who
nervously introduced her to his mother and then avoided
mentioning her ever again—when Sheila fled, she
crossed an ocean.

Because she had wanted to make her departure an act
of deliberation (trying to convince mostly herself),
Sheila took a freighter. No swimming pool, no shuffle-
board, no movies, no mixers, no library, no doctor, not
even a deck chair—all the way to tropical Malaysia. Islands, thousands of them. The destination mattered, but
not as much as the unhurried pace of travel, the com-
mitment to going. And then, to arriving. Twenty-seven
crew and a captain who spoke beautiful English, some
officers, four other passengers. To pass the days Sheila
walked. She walked upon waking. She walked one
deck, then the other, and each time she thought of
Chapman, she sneezed, violently. Later, oceans later, she
would find this funny.

At the beginning he called her Shee. He called her
Shee and tripped on the rug like an overexcited big
breed puppy. He once gave her a trilobite fossilized in
stone. If that wasn't deep love, then you tell me. Sheila
sneezed. The Filipino steward looked up. He knew
pain, in four languages. He made her tea but all he had
was pekoe. Sheila drank the pekoe and was grateful.

Sūrya Namaskār.

Sheila rose. She did sun salutations before dawn—
ten, twenty cycles—incorporating the standing poses
one by one as she recalled them until the sequence
lengthened to a string. *Tāḍāsana. Ūrdhva Hastāsana. Uttānāsana.* Mountain. Reach for the sky. Rag doll (fuck me).
*Adho Mukha Śvānāsana. Ūrdhva Mukha Śvānāsana. Adho
Mukha Śvānāsana.* Downward-facing dog, upward dog,
down dog. She held each pose, she closed her eyes. The
freighter cut through the skin of the ocean. She was
still, the ship was moving. The ocean was both still and
moving. *Trikoṇāsana.* Triangle, left and right. Everything
left and right. *Utthita Pārśvakoṇāsana.* Shoot like an arrow.
Vīrabhadrāsana I, II, III. Mighty warrior. *Ardha Chandrāsana.* Half-moon. *Parivṛtta Trikoṇāsana. Parivṛtta Pārśvakoṇāsana. Parivṛtta Ardha Chandrāsana.* Repeat the *asanas,*
with a twist. Breathing hard. *Uttānāsana.* Rag doll (oh,
fuck me). *Ūrdhva Hastāsana.* Reach for the sky. *Tāḍāsana.*
Mountain.

Sheila blinked. Albatross overhead, soaring. Nary a
flap. The wingspan of angels.

She closed her eyes. She began again.

Her heart was alive, she sweated, she faced east, from
where she came. Ten-minute yoga was a conceit, she
now understood. Wu knew, if one just got started, one
would not be able to stop after ten minutes. Yoga, like
true love, was the body reaching out in all directions,
one continuous expansion. Some kind of soaring.

Sheila rose. She walked. She walked before break-fast, she walked before lunch, clockwise, counterclock-wise, retracing in the afternoon the distance she gained in the morning. Her pace was unvarying, incantatory. In between, she read. She read, she stared at the ocean's plastic surface. Was only vaguely aware of dolphins surfing the bow. She could be in any ocean, the waters were unrelieved by any spot of land. She thought of Polynesians rowing double canoes no higher than their nipples, making their way to the blue beyond, and find-ing Tonga, Tahiti, the Hawaiian Islands; she thought of them with new awe. Were they lured by adventure, or driven out in peril?

After dinner, after the German captain had flirted brilliantly, dutifully, with her and with the wife of the podiatrist, Sheila excused herself and walked again. Al-ways she was polite in declining company. After eleven days of breeze and storm and sun and squalls, after eleven days during which she spoke less than a hun-dred words: land. Sheila got off. She had arrived at Osaka. She arrived at Osaka feeling not so much that she had sailed the ocean—but walked it.

Snow fell.

Sheila opened her hotel window. Snow fell in Kyoto.

A woman in a pleated skirt and beige overcoat rode by on a sturdy bicycle, holding an umbrella against the soft drift. White powder dusted the cars, the awnings, the roofs, the fanlike leaves on ginkos. Soon Sheila would have to leave Japan, leave or get a job. Two months, two days, and this one thing she's learned: Kyoto is laid out in a grid, no curved roads, no hills until you left the perimeter. One had to labor to lose oneself in this city. Sheila put on both sweaters, her thin jacket, over that, a shawl. She stepped outside, she lifted her head. Snow kissed her face.

In Kyoto, deep in the temple and gardens of Daitoku-ji is a modest pavilion. Take off your shoes, come in. Enter through the low doorway, *nijiriguchi,* enter on your knees. Crawl. Contemplate the shoji screens, the hand-made paper in the screens, the light wooden frames, the tatami that carpets the room, the sunken fire pit at the far end, which in turn holds a charcoal brazier. A woman in a double kimono is seated alongside. She bows, head to the tatami, hands just so. Bow in return. Her movements are reductive, ritualistic. She invites with a nod of the head, an extended arm: *please, sit.* Sit like her. Sit on your heels, back straight, hands resting in your lap. The tea maker welcomes you but does not look you in the eye. You are in the same room, but you are on your own. Breathe. Find in yourself a new rhythm. *Vīrāsana.* Hero pose.

The tea maker stirs the coals under the squat iron pot. The moon of her fingernail is black. A wayward ham-mer? A car door? Suddenly the woman possessed a hammer, a car, perhaps even a home, an untold story. Two gardeners come in from the frost, they bow to her, to you. Bow to them. They take off their hats and sit, they rub cold hands. A wet maple leaf is stuck to the pants of one. He puts it in his pocket. It leaves an imprint: I was here.

While the water in the cast-iron pot warms, contemplate these Japanese maples, red with leaf, edges crisp and browning, now heavier with snow. One leaf falls before another, a third one drifts, another swirls, and thousands of others cling to the branch by a grace finer than spider's silk. Contemplate the stone path that curved around and led unexpectedly, decisively to this humble pavilion. The fresh footprints you saw in the snow are yours. Contemplate the single rock set into thick, snowy moss, the depth of the well in that rock, the fine fall of water that filled this well into which you had immersed the bamboo dipper. Contemplate the clarity of the water, its welcome cold, as it washed over your hands. Think of Chapman, his hands, his fleet mind, his thigh between yours. Sneeze. Sneeze violently. Sneeze again. Laugh. You can.

Inside the tea pavilion hangs a bamboo vase holding a single white morning glory. Here are the instruments of the tea; here is this wild flower. That is all. Or, that is everything.

The water boils. The tea maker counts out three large black *raku* bowls, warms each with hot water, which she then discards. She wipes the rim of each bowl with precisely folded linen, *chakin*. She scoops green powdered tea, pours in a measure of boiling water, applies a bamboo whisk that has been split from a single joint of woody stalk, *chasen*. She whips the tea into a vivid green foam. The only sound is the breath of anticipation, the whir of her whisk. She sets out the bowls. One by one she presents the tea to each of her guests. She bows. Bow in return.

This is *cha*.

The gardeners take time to appreciate the tea, its fragrance, her artistry, her offering. They sip. The tea is a brilliant, hopeful green. Is bitter. The gardeners smile, content and more to be warmed, once with hands around their cups, and again with the exciting foamy liquid sliding down their throats. They sit, they cup their tea, they drink. They do not open mail, or make phone calls to their beloveds, they do not sob or argue with people in another house, another town, another country, as the woman at the tea pavilion in Daitoku-ji makes tea.

The gardeners finish. They return to work. They smile and bow. They leave on their knees. The tea maker has performed a service, she is fulfilled. She bows. In Japan, everyone bows and deeply, from the waist. It is a gesture at once formal and full of regard. The bankers who exchanged the last of Sheila's checks bowed. The kimonoed ladies in Ginza who sold her her bento box lunch bowed, as did the brilliantined marching band that passed her as she posted her letters home and the white-gloved conductor on the train that carried her in from Osaka to Kyoto. Now, as Sheila bows to the tea maker as she has seen the gardeners do—prostrate, from the waist, forehead to the mat, hands overhead just so, not unlike the deeply releasing child's pose, *Vīrāsana*—she realizes that bowing takes even less effort than making tea. One could think of it as a calling.

Fur

Fei Lo noticed the new clerk right away, a persimmon in a basket of oranges. Three letters on a gold-tone plaque spelled out her name. So as to make no mistake, the old gentleman wrote it in his notebook, *Fur.* He liked to know the names of all the women tellers, as he flirted with each in turn, even when his wife was alive. The clerks indulged him, they treated him with deference, they called him Ah Goong, Old Grandfather. Behind his back they said, and without derision, Fei Lo, Fat Man.

Fei Lo tipped his hat.

Fur said good morning, and she called him Ah Goong.

"Your name, very pretty."

She smiled. "I chose it myself."

Her mother had named her Sei Hèung, Four Fragrance. When American-born Chinese made fun of her nonsense name, she changed it to Fur, something she coveted more than any perfume. She tried first Mink, then Sable, but never Chinchilla, since it had too many syllables for Chinese. She finally settled on the all-encompassing Fur, and while it made no more sense than Four Fragrance, the other tellers let it go.

"Yes. Fur. Very distinctive."

Fur gave the old gentleman her full attention.

Fei Lo smiled, too.

He would offer a proposition, she only had to wait. "Something I can do for you today?"

Fei Lo could tell by the shift of her weight that she had stepped out of her shoes. He tapped his breast pocket where he kept his deposit.

"Guess," he said. "Guess the amount of my deposit, within 10 percent, and I will sign my check over to you."

Fur pressed her bunions back into her shoes; she rolled her tongue over her teeth. The clerks on either side stopped in midmotion but did not look up.

Backroom eavesdropping told her about the rotund flirt, his large appetites and even larger deposits—monthly totals of some $20,000 in Hong Kong rents, shack storefronts, $3 a square foot. She quickly calculated the 10 percent error and added a chunk. She did her best imitation of shooting in the dark.

"Oh, $23,199!"

Fei Lo's eyes narrowed. He glanced about. The other

women made busy. He did some calculating himself as he pulled out his check.

"Pretty good guess. But you are off about *15* percent."

"No! So close?? Let me see!" Fur examined the check before she stamped it. "Maybe next time I will be more lucky." She grinned.

"Ah. Maybe."

The next time Fei Lo came into the bank, Fur timed her transactions to coincide with his arrival at the head of the line. "Ah Goong, you are a traveled man. You ever been to Las Vegas?"

"Oh, many times. But Tahoe is nicer."

"Better than Vegas?"

"Umm. Like gold is better than paper."

"You win?"

"Win! Of course, win. Even when I lose, I win. Consider our hotel, very reasonable, very nice. Dining room—out of this world. Menu thick like a book, and every dish ready at your fingertips." He passed his hand over the counter so elegantly, Fur lifted up on her toes to see. "Lovely pink crab, prime rib, five different ways to eat potatoes—"

"—Any desserts?"

"On a table of their own! Meringue pies, sweet cream cakes—"

"—Chocolates?"

"Ah, chocolates. Yes, chocolates. Even on your pillow, chocolates."

Fur framed a smile and lowered her eyes. She could even blush on demand.

"Twelve dollars," he said. "All you can eat."

The bank clerk and the old man regarded each other. Between them, the teller's counter was laid end to end with food only they could see.

"I don't go anymore."

"Why not?"

"Wife died. She didn't like to go."

"Oh, sorry, Ah Goong. I didn't know." Fur knew. She had read his file. "But, Goong, what's to keep you, now that you are a free man?"

"No. Can't. It's no fun without her."

"Yeah, yeah, I understand."

Fei Lo reached into his breast pocket. He tried to keep it light. *"Néih séung mhséung heui?"* You want to go?

"Séung!" she said. "You bet. I'm going, yes, I am."

The bank clerk tilted her head toward a sign promoting the opening of new certificates of deposit, $1,000 minimum. "Twenty new accounts and I win a free trip." She winked. She drummed her fingernails, red painted over chipped.

Fei Lo turned away long enough to read the large print. "And how many you have so far?"

"Nineteen," she said, as if giving her age. He laughed out loud. The clerk on her right shot a glance, the one on the left harrumphed.

He pulled out his deposit and pushed the check to-ward her. She saw his knowing smile.

"Oh, no, Ah Goong, you get much more interest if you add this to your existing account. Oh, but you are such a kind man. Really, I mean it. Don't worry, before the day is over I will get my trip to Las Vegas. I'm a good salesman."

That threw him.

Fur keyed in his account number, then paused.

"Ah Goong, you want me to be happy?" She tapped the check on the counter.

Here it comes after all. "I want all you young women to be happy."

"You have been so kind to me, since the very first day. I want to take you to lunch. Will you let me, please?"

The bank clerk herded the fat man into the most expensive restaurant in Chinatown, one with valet parking and a doorman. Her eyes worked the room, studying, memorizing, the choice of wallpaper, the re-cessed lights, the antique screens—scholar on a donkey, painted silk in a teak surround.

"Oh, no, Ah Goong." She pulled the paper insert out of his hand. "No rice plate specials for you today. It's my birthday and we are having only the finest food on the menu. *"Oh! Yin wō!"* She lay her hand on his arm. "I've never had bird's nest soup. Can we have that? I mean, would you enjoy it?"

Fei Lo glanced at her hand. She removed it and giggled.

A fiftyish woman in a wool crepe suit bumped Fur's shoulder and made a point of apologizing. Fur never had a lady apologize to her, and this woman was deft. She managed within the same breath to greet her friends three tables away, tossing her hand in an effort- less wave. As she passed, Fur caught the surprise of her shoes, faux leopard with an open toe, the flash of cherry polish, as if a woman's power and every secret resided in the feet. Fur rubbed the top of her own pump against the back of her other leg, a quick dry polish under the table.

Fei Lo was staring at her. "So, how old are you today?"

"Oh! How old do you think I am?" She crossed her legs and leaned forward on her elbow. She giggled. She swung her free leg carelessly.

Fei Lo got a little warm. He giggled, too. He steadied his hands on the menu. He considered balance and contrast, spice and subtlety, texture, methods of prepa- ration, a soup, a fish, a fowl, some green vegetables to cleanse. He peered over his bifocals at her.

She flipped back and forth through the eight-page menu, her eyes scanning down the right-hand column as if doing addition. She smiled. "Remember, it's my treat."

It's my treat was repeated three more times during the meal they ordered as if it were a wedding banquet. Fei Lo was smitten to finally find a woman not afraid to eat. He didn't know Fur had not eaten since breakfast the day before, but he had already guessed that she couldn't afford such a meal on her salary and that, in the end, they both expected him to pay. By the time the oysters arrived sizzling, practically leaping, off the hot cast-iron plate, he had also deduced it wasn't really her birthday.

Fei Lo parked his Lincoln Continental next to the chapel, got his things out of the trunk, and started up the hill. He enjoyed the approach to the grave site and didn't want to rush. He liked the walking, the tulip beds in spring, the tall stalks of summer grass that stained the hems of his pants, proof of his participation. He liked reading the names on the houselike tombs, miniature temples adorned with columns. He, too, owned one of these stone houses, enough space for an extended family, guarded by an iron gate. If he drove up to the site, he might feel compelled to drop off the flowers and just go. Soon he might not come at all. Their children rarely came, at Christmas, her birthday, maybe Mother's Day, in alternating turns that smacked of arrangement.

He set his things down and used both hands to open his folding stool. He unlocked the gate and opened it wide, letting into the crypt every possible ray of sun. He hung his coat on the gate and said hello to his wife. "Hear that?" The crunch of leaves fueled his appetite. "Indian summer," he sighed. He sat down on the folding canvas.

From a plaid thermos he poured some fragrant hot tea. He fanned himself with the Chinese daily. When the tea cooled, he unwrapped the towel he used as insulation and untied the string around the square pink box, enough *dím·sām* for a family: parchment chicken, pink shrimp in translucent wraps, sweet rice studded with three treasures and bound with bamboo leaves, sweet black bean paste in a golden seeded pouch. From the tens of offerings from the *dím·sām* tray, Fei Lo always chose those that came wrapped up like gifts.

The sun warmed his back and he did not sweat. Fei Lo chewed his toothpick into a flat pulp. He didn't look at his wife's grave. With effort he could get through the entire visit without mentioning the bank clerk's unusual name, or the number of times they'd had dinner since the "birthday" lunch.

He held the newspaper upright and turned a bit away from the gate. This was not the way he had imagined it, him sitting here talking to her. The vision that came to him in the years before her death was of her, her coming with plants and flowering shrubs, working on hands and knees, she who would finally discover in widowhood the meditation of horticulture.

"Young Woo died last week," he relayed.

Young Woo was the seventy-three-year-old son of Old Woo, who was still living in his own home, in his own bed. Young Woo had built from a corner stand selling hand-knotted brushes a chain of hardware stores stretching up and down the peninsula. He made his father very comfortable. His last act was to step on wet dog excrement. Young Woo saw the droppings as he was taking the wheelchair from the trunk, and he was very careful while helping his father sit down. But a car backed into the space in front of him and banged his bumper. In his excitement, Young Woo let go of the wheelchair. It rolled, he lunged, he slipped, and broke his hip, from which he never recovered. Young Woo had built from nothing, yet this the ladies at the bank would soon forget, as quickly as they would forget his name, recalling only a man who was killed by dog droppings. Fei Lo unbuttoned his vest. He knew what men feared. Men feared acts of foolishness. Women had no trouble with this. They only feared being unvalued.

The air chilled.

The widower lifted his head just in time to see the last of the fall sunset, a pulsing ovoid tangent to the Pacific, the sky seared orange and red.

"What a fine view we have. A splendid view. Splendid."

Fei Lo watched until the colors bled from the sky.

"I'm looking for investors."

His children had warned him she would ask for money, it was just a matter of time. Fei Lo wanted to give it to her, whatever she asked. But his son said, "No." His daughter said, "No." They said, "We don't want it, Dad, but you need it to live on. And why do you want to give it to this woman with no family?" Fei Lo wondered how he could have raised such children. And yet, when a certain woman had asked Young Woo for a loan, Fei Lo had offered similar advice.

Fur laid her chopsticks across her rice bowl, she nudged her plate aside. She had barely eaten.

"Ah Goong, I'm not a clever person. Some people have good ideas every day. Me, I only have so many good ideas. Not every day. This is my good idea: a beauty shop for hair. No permanents. No color. No nails. Just wash and cut. Look, look at our beautiful hair."

Fur whipped out her drugstore compact and shoved the mirror under his nose. He had a view of the top of his head, spare gray strands parted low on one side and combed over to the other.

"Thick, straight, and black. The most desirable hair in the world. Why make it something different?" She snapped the compact shut and tapped it on the table. "Wash and cut." She amended as she went. "More than a cut, a shape, a frame for the face. A high-class." She inhaled with care. She looked him in the eye. "Partners. Fifty-fifty."

He stared at her, chopsticks poised. The rice was getting cold.

Fur wet her lips. "You like my idea, yes or no?"

Fei Lo hated talking business over food. He wished she had asked for fun money. He gladly would have given that, even a monthly allowance, whatever she wanted, for a little silk scarf, a sumptuous dinner, car payments. But this was an investment, and while the actual dollars might end up being the same, or even less, he had to think it out. Real estate he knew, but not shopkeeping. He asked himself, *Is it good business? Does she know about hair? Has she any talent?*

As if from behind his ear the bank clerk pulled out a card, the name of a salon, someone else's salon. "I'm there Thursday nights, all day Saturday, and Sunday until four." Whenever she wasn't at the bank.

Fei Lo considered Fur's own hair, which curiously enough was chemically curled and never struck him as anything special. But then he was no judge. He tried to calculate how many women would want their hair cut by her. Would his wife have gone to her? Would the ladies at the bank? And there came to him a startling realization. "Women don't like you."

He spoke with such carelessness, as if comparing coats in a store window, so that Fur, too, saw herself with detachment.

"That's right. Women don't like me. I don't fit, do I? But men like me fine. And men get their hair cut three times more often than women."

Fei Lo nodded. "Then what you really want is a barbershop."

"No, no, no. No barbershop. *Beauty* shop. Barbers charge a fraction what hairdressers charge." She marked off the tip of her index finger with her thumb to indicate how small a fraction she had in mind. "Barbers don't wash. I wash. I wash very good, very gentle. Men like that. You come sometime, I show you."

They stared at each other.

Fei Lo thought about more shrimp, salty, crusty, pan-fried little devils on their bed of lettuce.

Fur let her gaze wander about the room. She tinked her glass with her chopsticks. When the waiter approached, she got up to go to the rest room.

Fei Lo caught her eye. "Let me think about it."

She nodded once and smiled, knowing that he wouldn't.

The bank clerk made a detour by the bar and talked to three different men, men she knew well enough to touch their shoulders. There was laughter, eyes that did not move, glancing hands, codes he had long forgotten.

When she continued on to the bathroom, the men watched through half-closed lids. Heads inclined in her direction. Someone made a joke. They all laughed.

Fur took her time returning. Fei Lo stood up and held out her chair, but she did not sit. She slipped on her jacket and said, "I should take you home now. It's a long drive for me back to Fremont."

"But, I can take a cab. Please, sit down, we haven't finished our dinner."

"Oh, no, I couldn't let you take a cab. You are my dearest friend. I'll wait. Please. Sit down. Eat."

She sat and did not look about, did not eat, did not fidget. She was more silent than even his wife had been on her most quiet days.

Fei Lo lost appetite. He didn't ask for the leftovers.

They drove, and the silence sat between them like cold fat. Chinatown blurred into downtown, which blurred into the lakefront—man-made, polluted, and fringed with high-rises. A wall of glass separated them from a cocktail party halfway up a building, sparkling stemware, red wine and white. Below them a family ate in silence. Another tasted from cartons passed back and forth. Others were locked down for the night in front of TVs that etched them in a pulsing blue light. On the top floor, darkness, except for one low light, a night-light.

As their car rounded the bend, Fei Lo could make out a form. A child too young to stay alone pressed her palms into the glass and kissed her own reflection.

"Is it true, what they say about your father?" And as soon as the words came out, he regretted.

Fur tapped the brakes. "Who, they? What do they say?"

"The women at the bank. They say—" Fei Lo blushed. "They say your father had two wives."

The women had circulated a story about young Four Fragrance, some said twenty, some said eighteen. One woman said she was barely fourteen, with a dead mother and the address in America of a father she had never met. They spiced it up with his car, all fins and angles, his quick drive-up to the curb, a hand that reached out only to slap her face, the motor running. They iced it with his parting line, "I have no daughters. Don't call me again."

Fur said nothing and Fei Lo wondered if she had heard him. She drove straight to his house without instruction, pulled up the curved driveway, and parked behind his garaged Lincoln Continental. She killed the engine and looked out at nothing in particular.

"Rumors, Ah Goong, are like the bamboo. Planted and left alone, they will multiply into a forest that blocks out all light. They weave a root system you cannot destroy. The tiniest splinter can cause unbearable pain. And every day the bamboo sways, it bangs one into its neighbor. It wails its song, it clanks its tune, and makes you deaf to all other music."

She turned and smiled at him. "Or so my mother used to tell me. You believe this?"

They sat some. The windows fogged.

He asked, "You want to come in?"

She didn't answer but when he came around and opened her door, she got out.

Fur sat cross-legged on the bathroom carpet, reading dated decorating magazines. Her eyes stopped on an advertisement of metal spiral staircases. She tore out the page and tossed it with other torn sheets, ragged ideas for a dream salon.

Fei Lo was a few steps away when he thought he heard something rip. He tapped the door. "Is everything all right?"

She didn't answer.

He unlocked the bar and set out his favorite liqueurs, substituting brandy for port and French for domestic until he felt he got it right. He went back and asked if she would like a drink. She turned a page and said without shouting, "I can't hear you. I'll be out soon."

When Fur finally emerged, the TV was on. Fei Lo had fallen asleep, his head hung on his chest. A fire raged in downtown San Francisco. Glass exploded. A barefoot woman half in flames stumbled from the building. The fire seized her like a jealous husband. Fur nudged the old man with her finger. His lips fluttered.

She walked along his mahogany bookcases, dragging that same finger along the shelves. No dust. Even now, though *she* was dead, no dust. Not many books either, some statement in simplicity. But each spare shelf was anchored by an object, things *she* probably picked out.

Above the bar was a pair of jade lions, one facing east and one west. She picked one up and nearly dropped it. Much too heavy to slip into a pocket. On another shelf—arranged so precisely as to discourage touching—what looked like shoehorns. Fur flipped one over. They *were* shoehorns. Here, in the front room. Carved ivory, no two alike, untouched by human feet. A pair of this, a dozen of that, nothing was collected singly, as if Fei Lo's wife had been shoring up against a day of enormous need. Fur understood that urge.

Here, sterling bowls, graded to nest, so shiny with polish they sang. The hollows of each were lacquered a different color—ruby, emerald, sapphire. Fur pulled a bobby pin from her hair, chewed off the coated tip, and ran the sharp end against a ruby hollow. She was surprised to find that it did scratch. She glanced at Fei Lo, then wet a finger with saliva and tried to repair the damage. She shrugged, picked up another. This bowl was filled with chocolates, individually wrapped in foil and molded into assorted seashells. Fur put a fat fistful in her pocket and continued her tour of Fei Lo's house, saving the master bedroom for last.

There she was, Fei Lo's dead wife, captured as a young woman of forty, sitting in the shade of a backyard tree, framed for all eternity in sterling. Even seated, the woman looked uncommonly tall. Fur flopped down in the middle of the bed. She wondered what kind of woman would wear a suit in her own backyard.

Two doors flanked the oversize bed. One led to Fei Lo's closet, the other to an enormous walk-in, perhaps once a study or a nursery, and finally refitted as a temple of adornment. On either side of the windows were identical built-in dressers, gloss white with cut-glass pulls. Opposite was a matching cabinet for shoes, shoes for every season and every social occasion, including shoes in which to be alone in the house. Handmade of fine leather, not one pair would try a woman's balance, or redefine the toes, or hinder flight from a difficult situation.

Fur stepped in. She opened drawers, she fingered lingerie several sizes too large. Around her neck she wound a rope of pearls.

On the vanity lay an engraved silver tray laid out with everything a woman needed to enhance, mask, or preserve. She picked up a crystal atomizer and misted behind each ear, then tried to fan away the sticky perfume. *Bedazzle, Promise*—lipsticks that gave no clue to their color but attested to some state of mind. She wiped off her own lipstick and drew a new mouth. The vivacious pink favored by older women barely covered lips stained dark red. The corners of her mouth where the tissue had missed formed sharp little brackets around her smile. She looked all wrong and told herself it was lovely.

Initials were carved into the matching brush. Fur tossed her hair. *One, two, three . . . one hundred strokes a day for a dazzling shine.* In the dusty gutters between the bristles, the hairs of two women matted into a loose felt. Fur rested her forehead against the mirror. When the glass warmed, she rolled her forehead to the next cool spot. She opened her eyes. Pink lips, so close to her own they almost touched. She leaned, much less effort than holding the distance. She pressed her lips against the glass.

When she turned to go, she saw it.

In the back of two long racks of dresses—a zippered cotton bag. Dark brown hairs poked through the neck and glistened. Fur walked over. She unzipped. There it was, Fei Lo's dead wife's coat, mink past the knees.

The gold paper was stamped with a pattern of ridges and spines, a miniature nautilus wrapped around dark imported chocolate. Unlike cheap candy that clawed and irritated, this confection slipped down the throat and satisfied.

The gold paper was subtly textured and, like fine damask, when angled just so to the light, it revealed secret designs—diamonds—iridescent and intermittent. Opened flat, the foil was about a three-inch square. It never failed to amaze Fei Lo how boxes and bags could be knocked down to a flat piece of hard paper with notches and missing corners. But the spines that formed this shell design could not be flattened. They were hot-stamped into the paper almost permanently, giving the wrapped chocolate its crisp elegance. Fei Lo turned the foil over. A shard of chocolate fell free from the crease. He stared at it before tapping it into his mouth.

In the restaurant, he would watch his daughter fold the long, flat envelope her chopsticks came in, first twice along its length, then diagonally across one end. She would turn the paper over and fold, turn, and fold, butting one crease up against its neighbor, a process that gave the paper thickness and integrity. Then she would hook the ends together and make a ring on which to rest her chopsticks. She made one for him and one for herself, her fingers busy while they discussed the menu. He had watched her do this many times, and still he could not duplicate the process.

He tried it now with this square of gold foil, knowing the proportions were wrong and his fingers no longer deft. He inhaled, his breath whistled, but he refused to breathe through his mouth. Only children, asthmatics, and dying dogs breathed through their mouths. He also refused to talk to himself. He would not do that. So it was largely in silence, broken by his whistling breath, that he folded and refolded the gold paper, patiently trying to transform a flat square into a standing ring, as he waited for Fur to call.

It was Thursday when he found the foil, almost two weeks after their last dinner. The gold paper lay scrunched in the hallway outside his daughter's old bedroom, a room last used by his wife as her private refuge. She could have sat in their raked rock garden, or in the living room overlooking the creek, but she preferred to spend her afternoons in her daughter's old room, which faced east and was cool. What she did in there he never asked, and she never volunteered. He occasionally passed the door just after she went in. If he shut his eyes, a pattern of sound would return: the pull of a paper shade, a book scraping the shelf, a lamp switch at midday.

He wouldn't have stopped outside the door, but there was this piece of litter, this scrap of gold. He bent over, and from that stooped position he saw light under the door in a room unvisited except by the housekeeper.

Fei Lo opened the door. It wasn't the overhead, but a table lamp in the middle of the room. He walked over in such a hurry to walk out again, he was already turning away even as he reached for the switch. The hot socket stung. He recoiled and slipped on something slick—opened books, half shoved under the club chair.

"What the goddamn."

Afraid of moving his feet, Fei Lo leaned on the table and set his considerable weight on his forearm. He turned the light up another notch. More books lay on the carpet, almost as if arranged.

Fur.

In here. She had been in here. Fei Lo turned as if he heard a thief. But—not just in here. She had gone into every room of his house. He could imagine her, nosing around, touching everything, here, where his child used to sleep, her eyes eating up whatever they wanted, while he slept, while he snored, the greedy hussy. What has she ever wanted that he had not given? He wanted to ask, *What kind of girl you are, you come into my house and look while I sleep?* Was it too late to call? He called. Her phone rang rang rang. Had he slept with his mouth open? He angled his watch to the light. Ten P.M. He hung up and redialed. Hung up again. Call the police. He laughed. And tell them what? That she ripped up some magazines? That she dared to sashay in here in her, her *sa chahn* way, here where his wife had always shut the door. Fei Lo took out his handkerchief and wiped his forehead. Robbed. He was sure of it. His son was right. His daughter was right. Surely, she had taken something.

He walked around until he was standing where he

imagined her sitting. But, he was mistaken. Photo albums, not books. He traced the trail back to the book-
case, shelves tight with albums, a rack as high as a
hatted man, as wide as a marrying couple.

The old man slumped into the overstuffed chair, then
reflexively jerked his feet back, as if at the last moment
he saw her sitting here, cross-legged on the floor, her
skirt riding up, surrounded by these musty photographs—birthday parties, horses, a succession of bigger
houses and better neighborhoods. And when her legs
became numb, she had stood up and stretched. While
he slept in the front room, she had kicked off her shoes,
tucked naked legs under, and sat, in this same chair, in
this very room, where his daughter shut the door, where
she talked in hushed tones with girlfriends, where his
wife used to nap, where the two of them brushed each
other's hair while his son wheeled around on his tricycle, head back, hairs flying behind, caught forever in
the streak of being two years old.

Funny, Fei Lo couldn't remember his son having a
tricycle. But every child had a tricycle.

He got out his glasses. He pulled the lamp close and
sat down. The album was edge-stitched with brown
yarn. Roy Rogers waved from his horse and smiled the
So long smile. Fei Lo wiped the cover with a handkerchief, sneezed, and turned the page. A square of foil
slipped out. And another. A cascade of gold.

He dropped the book.

He stood up faster than his blood could recover and he lumbered across the room. The door frame boxed him. Seal it up. Let the housekeeper tidy it. He slammed the door so hard it popped open again. Fei Lo steadied himself in the dim hall.

In time, the eye adjusts. Pupils dilate. A table lamp and a comfortable chair were what he saw. That's all. Together they defined a space and scale for intimacy. Yes, he could imagine them in there, his daughter, his wife, even Fur. Nothing had happened. She had been looking, only looking. It could just as easily have been like that.

If there were ten albums on the floor, there were another eighty or ninety still on the shelves, no two alike. The books on the top shelf documented the youth of his wife, until she married; then she almost disappeared. There were few pictures of him or of the two of them, fewer yet of the entire family. And what pictures there were of the four of them showed events he could little recall, as if his participation had been aural and after the fact.

Here—something familiar. On their wedding day, his mother had broken her foot and his brothers jostled for the privilege of carrying her. *Her* mother was relieved to find for her gangly daughter a decent and equally tall husband. He turned the page. His bride could not believe how skinny he was coming from such ample parents.

And after she had gotten used to skinny, she could not believe how quickly he could grow. With each return trip to Hong Kong, he would multiply their wealth (hers), and come back displaying it to the world around his middle. That day, she had loved him handsome in a top hat, and said he should own one. With that passing remark, she had inspired in him a taste for acquisition as a measure of his feeling for her. That day, he had kissed her for the first time.

Fei Lo had to rest his eyes.

Over the years he had perfected the habit of falling asleep in his chair, to awaken refreshed after everyone had gone to bed. Then, in the company of other people's sleep, he would pad about the house, eating whatever he wanted, wherever he wanted, admiring figurines he suspected were new, thumbing through textbooks lying about, arranging the shoes at the front door into tidy pairs.

After the children left and after his wife died, he was at liberty to roam the house. He stayed up later and later, to bed at dawn, to table at three. Soon he could not distinguish night from day. He feared a tumor. His doctor laid a hand on his shoulder and said it was grief, and would pass.

Christmas, 1962. His wife posed in her new ranch mink, the top of her head cut off, her eyes red from the flash, making her seem alien. He had admired her coat when she had come to pick him up. "You like it? I picked it up on my way home from the airport. Perhaps it could be my Christmas present?" Each year he returned three, four times to Hong Kong, to inspect their properties, to visit their mothers. But he only ever missed that one Christmas.

He thought he had seen his wife last week, in San Francisco, going up the alleylike Commercial Street. Or rather, her mink coat. From the back, a woman walking away, in a fur coat, and on a fairly mild day. The warm weather and the coat's vague familiarity distracted him, because the walk he knew very well. He had spent many evenings watching Fur walk away.

Fei Lo slipped a finger beneath his bifocals and rubbed. He knew without having to check his wife's closet.

A fur coat. She wanted a fur coat. For a damn coat she made herself into a thief.

Dinner, she had written. *Next Saturday. Someplace new. All you can eat.* Then she had kissed him before leaving. He could just taste her lipstick when he woke.

Dusk. Thousands of amber lights came up in the special stillness that occurs only in dead winter. The city shimmered.

Of all the views of this city, Fei Lo loved best this one

at night from Treasure Island. He thrilled in the quick exit from the bridge as other drivers braced for the tunnel. From the island, the city's spires seemed to rise straight out of the bay. These buildings were set upon precious square footage and thrown up to the skies, maximizing the total number of rooms that could command rent. Under these towers lay a scattering of buildings scaled more for mortals. One of them was new and sprawling, built in flagrant disregard of cost.

With reluctance Fei Lo got back on the bridge and continued on to San Francisco. He drove three times around the same block until a street spot opened up, all the while half hoping for failure and an excuse to go home.

A single restaurant occupied the entire new structure, a building so flat and expansive it spread out like a stain, this restaurant launched by a Hong Kong entrepreneur eager to reinvest, eager to put both the Empress and the Mandarin to shame. Every lavishness had been pursued. That was the talk. And to guarantee good fortune, the owner had staged a parade, he hired a dragon, he chose a name of promise and called it The Forbidden Palace.

Fei Lo hated this kind of restaurant, where overplush carpets absorbed all gaiety, where autographed pictures defined who you weren't, and men felt more at ease without their families. Gloved waiters served with discretion. Deals were negotiated in a subtle mélange of tranquillity and artful consumption. Right hands clasped, left hands remained on the table. Why come to a restaurant if not to eat? Yet he attended the grand opening and returned each subsequent Saturday night, arriving early, staying late, eating, drinking, hoping for a glimpse, a chance encounter to set Fur straight.

But opening night belonged to the wife, the mother of the owner's sons. The following Saturday, to the owner's favorite mistress, not the youngest, but the most ruthless. With each succeeding week, Fei Lo had felt both a petty victory and some small embarrassment for Fur, whose one claim in the hierarchy was to be novel.

Tonight he should have stayed home. Or gone to the Economy Cafe in Oakland run by a Chinese granny sporting dark glasses to filter out what the grill on the windows could not. For a fraction of what he would be leaving here for a tip, he could have had a bowl of granny's fine *jūk*. The rice soup soothed as it meandered through one's system, happily carrying away with it all impurities. His stomach was in need of rest.

Fei Lo arranged and rearranged his utensils. From a deposit slip, he tried once again to fold a paper ring, ignoring the ceramic one that matched in design the plates and bowls and the solid brass door handles. He canted the chopsticks—here, ebony.

He was tired and was contemplating leaving, going home to lie down, just getting up and going, now, before the waiter arrived—when Fur finally walked in.

She was preceded by the men in tuxedos, the owner and his towering guards. Fei Lo knew S.K., a man of questionable alliances on both sides of the Pacific. During the Japanese War, he had tried to buy up a quarter-mile section of Tsim Sha Tsui, including property once owned by Fei Lo's wife.

S.K. conferred with his men; his eyes swept the room. He pointed with discretion and the young men nodded as one. The group moved on, leaving Fur standing all alone. And yet she continued to wait for one of the men to come back, to help her out of her coat, to hand it to the checker, this fur that had belonged to an Amazon of a Cantonese and that she clutched to her breast as if it protected against some as yet undiscovered element.

Fei Lo went past the bar, past the bank of telephone booths, past several doors marked PRIVATE, and down the broad, curving stairs, following arrows that pointed the way. On the door to the men's room was a hand-lettered sign: *The management regrets ... Please, use the ladies' room.* Fei Lo could hear voices, arguments about specifications and fulfillments punctuated by banging pipes and gurgling water. He added music of his own as he turned away—his shoes squished the carpet.

The door to the ladies' room was propped open. Fei Lo hesitated. His intestines insisted. Room opened onto room, opened onto room. He looked up and was startled to see a sickish old man, equally startled, staring back at him. He was standing in a generous powder room faced with enormous sheets of silvered glass, floor to ceiling and wall to wall. Relief came where one expanse of mirror was sheared by a slab of peach-veined marble. Fei Lo was now supporting his gut with his hand. He shouldn't have ordered for two, shouldn't have then tried to eat it. A man came out of the washroom after first allowing some women to pass. It seemed all right to go in.

He rushed through the washroom to the toilet room and locked himself in the first free cabinet. Despite the warm tones and textured wallpaper, he still felt the chill and damp.

By the time Fei Lo finished, the washroom had emptied out. He removed his jacket and hung it on a shiny brass hook.

The hall door creaked open and swung shut.

"Don't turn around."

Fur was standing in the outer room so that only her reflection could be seen. His heart tightened. In the mirror she seemed so far away.

The old man worked the pink soap into a lather. "Why not turn?"

She tried to make it light. "I have to fix my slip."

Without her coat, he could see she had lost weight. He missed her fleshiness, the suggestion of abundance.

Her smart black sheath and stilettos only heightened her gaunt frame. She looked worn, as if from the strain of standing erect.

"Are you well?"

She waited until he looked up again. "Why didn't you stop me?"

He purposely misunderstood. "But, you were with your party."

Fur arranged and rearranged a wayward curl. "He's asked me to marry him."

"Congratulations."

Neither of them mentioned the golden anniversary wife, the litter of mistresses.

"Do you love him?"

Her smile was a fine-line crack in her face. "Did you marry for love? What do you and I know about it? You've been in America too long."

Fei Lo paled. He leaned heavily against the sink, seized by sharp pains in his gut. Fur started toward him, but she wasn't used to helping. She didn't know where to begin. When he straightened up, she busied herself with the contents of her purse.

She finally blurted out, "What about the coat?"

Fei Lo cupped some water to his mouth. "Your fur coat? It looks very nice on you."

"Don't be a fool. It's not *my* fur coat."

He had to laugh.

"Aren't you going to call the police?"

"And say to them what?"

"Your wife's coat has been stolen!"

There. She said it. Almost. But where was the satisfaction? Fei Lo wet his handkerchief and applied it to the back of his neck.

"To call the police I would first have to go home to my wife's closet, where I never go, and discover that her fur coat is missing."

Fur's eyes darted here and about. Everywhere she looked she could see only herself. "You won't go into her closet?"

It had never occurred to him that his death could be sudden. He could very well die tonight. Even right here, down in S.K.'s basement toilet. No one would remember the fortune he had built, from nothing, shacks. They would remember only another old man who died without his family.

"In order to find the coat is missing, I would have to violate my wife's sanctuary. I would have to think of my friend as a thief. And I would have to consider myself indifferent to a life I can't fully comprehend. That would be the cost to me." He looked for the towel dispensers and found in their place monogrammed linens. "And the gain? I might get back a coat my wife can't wear, a coat my daughter won't wear. A political coat, she says." He tossed his towel in a basket. "Besides, it's not the coat that I miss."

The hall door opened. A young man filled the frame.

He glanced at Fur. She was drawing a generous outline around her lips. The man moved through the wash-room, through the toilet room, the snap of heels, the bang of doors. Down the aisle. Back. Fei Lo managed to produce a comb. Fur was filling in her lips with a sable brush, an even darker shade of red than she used to wear. She puckered. She blotted. The young man paused at the door.

"Five minutes," he said, and he left without haste.

Fur was flush with color, as if the threat excited. All these weeks Fei Lo had mistakenly thought his desperation to find her was to chastise.

"Fur, you are the boss. Of your own life, you are the boss." If only they were in the same room. "Please, learn to make better opportunities."

"Opportunity! Always the deal! You and he were cut from the same womb—you think I'm a deal to be made?"

Fei Lo shook his head. "Please. I meant no disrespect." He wanted to lie down. "What do I know of fancy words? I just want for your happiness."

She tossed her tissue and kissed the air in front of her. "Maybe it's not just *my* happiness that concerns you."

Fei Lo blushed. "Oh! You are an impossible girl! S.K. will ruin you. Without regret!"

"I have a top-floor apartment, a view of the Golden Gate so wide I have to turn my head to see. He visits two or three times a month. I regret nothing."

"And your name is on the deed?"

She gave no answer.

"You have a driver? Wherever you go, he goes?"

"I live like an empress."

"An empress is *protected* by those who watch her."

"And with you life could be so different?"

"Yes! Of course different, because *I* am different."

"Here's how you are different. You hang on to all those shacks in Tsim Sha Tsui when you could have bought in Victoria, like S.K., be a millionaire many times over."

His color deepened. "Anyone can take valuable property and turn a profit. Where is the challenge in that? I have taken what others discard as worthless and made that into something valuable."

"I am no chunk of land to be improved. I am not worthless. I will not be discarded."

"No. Of course not." Fei Lo leaned on the sink. He went back over their times together and thought of all the things he might have done differently, yet he was unwilling to give up hope, or the desperate optimism one can acquire in increasing abundance the nearer one gets to the end of life.

As if she could read his mind, she said, "Nothing you do will change things."

"What I do is of no consequence, you are right. But what you do can determine the rest of your life."

"Mine is a good life, Ah Goong. No better." She spoke with little conviction.

"I fear you will beat me to the grave."

From a wealth of names, *gā·jē, múi, gū·mā, bíu·jé*—precise nouns that left no question whether a sister was older or younger, a cousin was male or female, an aunt single or not, related by blood or marriage, and on which side of the family—from the hundred names that defined the exact relationship between two family members, he could find not one that might describe how he felt about her. And yet he had come to think of Fur as family.

"We could have had something fine, something that honored us both, a relationship not unlike what I had with my wife, or daughter, or sister, or even my mother. Something—fundamental."

Fur snapped her tiny clutch.

Fei Lo flinched.

She avoided his gaze, steadfast and genuine, but she could not avoid the ring of his words: *sister, daughter, wife. Something fine,* he said. *Something fundamental.* Something, she felt, completely foreign to them both. He might as well have invited her to jump off the boat. For what?

The minutes ticked. Four. Five.

Wife, sister, daughter—if she could hold still, the brilliance would surely fade.

Her voice was barely audible. "I'm a good girl, Ah Goong. You believe me?"

He nodded. She did not see.

"I was a fool to take the coat. And you had invited me into your home."

Fei Lo's heart caught.

Fur stepped into the doorway, a little unsteady. Her determination remained, but not the steel. He could imagine her in the center of other cold rooms, awkward, young, toughing it out, coached from the side by a mother who forced her child to practice standing alone.

Fei Lo shifted to turn.

Fur held a finger to her lips, at once kiss and admonition: *Don't...turn.*

He ached to turn.

She moved toward the door. It squeaked. Fur stepped through.

Fei Lo would not remember going up to the street, nor would he remember the people he passed, any more than they would remember him. He would recall instead the lightness of her steps.

Fei Lo climbed the stairs and stopped only when he reached the sidewalk. The stars seemed especially bright and plentiful tonight. Not a cloud in the sky. Not even a wisp.

He had to smile. All these years he had been gazing at the skies at the wrong time of day, so dazzled was he by the sun, so thankful for its warmth on his back. All those nights he had knocked about his house while his family slept, he could just as easily have stepped outside his door and looked up. Bāk Dáu Chāt Sīng, Sīn Hauh Chóh, the Big Dipper, Cassiopeia, the stars were the same no matter what they were called, constant in the firmament, whether or not he looked, there to give definition to the space that could be seen, and hint at what could not.

Fei Lo shielded his eyes from the streetlights and counted, taking special delight in the smallest, faintest sparks, stars that might indeed be small, but could just as easily dwarf his sun while being much farther away. So far away that some already may have burned out even though their light was just now reaching his eyes. So far away that numbers were incomprehensible. So far away that faith was prerequisite.

He counted all the stars that he could see, and when he was finished, he felt confident that if he stood there a bit longer he would spot another. And another. The price for such clarity was just the cold, the pure cold of a clear night. Fei Lo paused to savor its kiss and sting.

Her Slow and Steady

When the storm came unannounced, Bert cut short a construction visit and headed out of the city. All around, the fog was thick. It swallowed whole cars, the far end of his light beams. It sat on his hood, it butted his glass. Bert wiped the inside of the windshield with his hand and laughed. He might as well be driving with his eyes closed.

He was inching across the Golden Gate Bridge, named not for the International Orange of its paint, nor for the gold that had been mined in the foothills beyond (and by his pigtailed countrymen), but for the strait that it spanned—a mile-wide squeeze through which the waters from the formidable San Francisco Bay met head-on those of the relentless Pacific. Chrysopylae, or Golden Gate, the strait was named by Frémont after the Golden Horn inlet of the Bosporus, valued for its brevity in linking Asia to the Western world.

By sea it was easy to miss. The Europeans had all
sailed past the fog-guarded entry, even Drake. Discovery took another two hundred years and a lost party. It
took a blue-sky day and men on foot, on horseback, to
find this strait and the wealth of the bay. The Spanish
explorers were picking their way through jagged,
forested cliffs when the land came to an abrupt stop.
They pulled their horses up short and stared at the
north shore a mere mile away. Between it and them lay
a bay of staggering dimension, with fingers reaching so
far inland it thwarted both the eye and the imagination.
Bert thought how daunting the bridgeless bay must
have seemed, because it was not the habit of explorers
to be deterred.

A gap in the fog, the *erk* of brakes, a flare of red
lights. Bert stopped in time but heard behind him the
beginning of a chain reaction. The fog closed up again.
He thought he felt the bridge sway, though it was hard
to be sure without points of reference. He inched on.
Visibility was, at best, an idea to revere—like the exis-
tence of a higher being. Bert marveled at the confidence
of pilots.

Water flared from beneath the tires in a cab-reaching
V. From the smell of cow piss, he guessed he was some-
where between Meerje's ranch and Poole's. Middle Two
Rock was already under water, as was Grace's road where

it finally crossed into unincorporated territory. The sign at the right said COUNTY MAINTAINED ROAD ENDS, and it did. He braked the truck to a crawl, which was about as fast as anyone ever drove up this gutted lane, even on a dry day. The road was already sloppy and he wondered if he would make it home before it turned to *jūk*.

He continued with his head out the window, mindful of snapped branches. Half a mile later, the twisty climb gave way to a clearing, a struggling cedar, and their L-shaped wood frame house. Having pushed hard to get home quickly, he now just sat in the truck.

They had met while he was dating her younger sister. When Grace said *Stan who?* he had whisked both sisters off to the amphitheater on top of Mount Tamalpais. Stan Getz strode on with his saxophone, waved, played an affecting set, smiled, waved, and walked off. Even as her husband was restraining her, the woman next to Bert jumped up and shouted, "Stan, I love you, Stan. I want to marry you. I'll be so good." Grace smiled elegantly and noted that she couldn't have said it better.

Bert shouldered the door against the wind. Grace was sitting in the cold and dark not even pretending to turn the pages of her book. He flipped the switch. He flipped all the switches. Nothing came on. The valley was grayed as far as he could see. This could be a three-day rain. He should have stopped for groceries.

In one motion he grabbed a kitchen towel and stepped out of sodden shoes. He wiped down his hair.

From beneath the cloth, he caught a glimpse of her bare feet.

"Hi," he said.

"Bert," she answered slowly, as if to remind herself who he was.

It was colder in the house than it was outside, yet she was wearing this gauze of a dress. Bert recalled that it had started out as a sunny day, a late Indian summer day. He himself had gone off without a jacket. He went to change. Maybe she would light the fire, now that he was home.

In midmorning on that June day, Grace had left Lucy asleep to take a quick shower. When she came back to check, Lucy's face was pressed awkwardly against the side of the bassinet and she was no longer breathing. Grace dropped to her knees naked and dripping, pinched the baby's nose, and forced air into her mouth. Like this she worked, long after even she realized it was futile. When Bert raced home an hour later, he found the two of them on the veranda, Lucy flaccid in her mother's lap as Grace played the naming game with the baby's toes: Christina, Wilhelmina, Ekaterina, Nefertiti, Nāhi'ena'ena, Elizabeth, Leia, Sacajawea, Scheherazade, and Our Lucy Ching. That day, Grace had merely touched each toe in turn, rocked and rocked her baby, and said not a word. The day after they buried her, Bert went outside to escape the quiet and found Grace on the porch, squeezing the milk from her breasts. Lucy had lived three months, long enough to learn to smile. In time, the milk stopped coming.

Grace lay her book down and drifted over to the woodstove. Her hands were so cold it hurt her to touch anything. She tore newspapers into strips and built a nest. From kindling she made a log cabin.

On their second date she had taken Bert to hear André Watts at the Paramount Theatre, when Calvin Simmons was conducting the then new Oakland Symphony with his infectious delight, when Calvin Simmons was young with promise and not yet drowned. Mr. Watts sang while he played the Emperor Concerto, his body swaying all over the keyboard while his behind was nailed to the piano bench. Bert's eyes lingered on the man's face, where every minute thing Mr. Watts felt about the music seemed to pass. Out of respect, Bert looked away. Grace had no trouble looking.

"You squeezed my hand," he whispered.

"*Haih ma?*" Really?

The next morning, Bert saw a picture of André Watts in the local paper. Mr. Watts said he felt funny playing in front of strangers—*unnatural* was the word he used—because making music is a very intimate experience. Private. Bert understood private. Getz was like that, private. Loving was private.

Grace struck a match. The newspapers whooshed

into flames. Minutes later the splinters glowed red-orange before curling back toward the wood.

Bert walked straight to the bathroom and stripped down. His feet were white with cold. When he opened the lid to the washer, he smelled more than saw the damp load clinging to the sides of the drum. It would have to be rerun. He got in the shower, hoping Grace might join him. She didn't. He wrapped himself in a towel and felt his way to the bedroom. Without lights, it was easy to avoid looking into the nursery.

Inexplicable phenomenon. Grace had leaned over at the prenatal lecture and whispered, "That's doctors' Latin for *don't know.*" They couldn't help joking about SIDS that night, grasping at levity in two hours of learning everything that could possibly go wrong. Now that sudden infant death syndrome had happened to them, they wanted to know. She did. Every study, every statistic, every new theory about crib death. But Bert understood. Some things cannot be explained.

Now, Getz dying—that could be explained. The man had had problems with drugs. He was sixty-four. And, there was the cancer. But how could Bert explain Calvin Simmons going out in a canoe at dusk without a life jacket, when he didn't know how to swim? Had he been teasing the gods? Bert had seen it before, on Alice

Street, that first summer he lived in the States. Two boys hid between the parked cars and the rubbish, and played a fast game of chicken: how late could they jump out in front of a moving car and not be hit? Bert was practicing his calligraphy, as he had promised his mother he would continue to do, when the first driver sat on his horn and laid down a hot stink of rubber. The boys ran clear into Chinatown with their hearts in their throats, laughing and choking on their own spit. *Now you.* Bert was still leaning out his window when Now You was thudded into the air some distance before he fell and ruptured his disks on the hood ornament of a '55 Chevy. Was that what Mr. Simmons was doing, leaping out in front of speeding gods? Two women witnessed the drowning on the lake. A sudden wind, a canoe out of control. One dived into the frigid waters, the other stroked out in her kayak. They reached an empty boat, spinning, spinning.

From the bedroom, Bert brought her a sweater and a pair of his own wool socks. She thanked him and set them on the arm of her chair. He needed a sign and found it in the smudges on her hand.

"How did it go today?"

"Finished the west elevations."

"Good. Great." Plans not only had to be finished, but

approved. Trees ordered and delivered. It was already November. He took a deep breath. Still, it was a solid start. And, she had started the fire.

Bert lit storm lamps, then sat down to make a list. If the house was burning down, he would make a list, a mental list, but still a list. Her slow and steady man, Grace called him. Once, their house almost did burn down. Bert had smelled the fire before he could see the smoke. A freak wind out of the Gulf of Mexico, two thousand acres of crisp yellow grass. All afternoon Bert and Grace had watched the fire advance and Bert re-fused to evacuate. Grace and Aaron, who was Bert's best friend and partner, had tried to coax him into the truck. "I'm not leaving," he said. "I'm not giving up my home." Aaron said, "Trees are fuel." He said, "Smoke in-halation." He said, "Only one road out." Bert pushed a screwdriver deep into the wood of the porch post. "Look at this house, Aaron. Infested, heatless, uninsu-lated—you know, if it's spared, I might just have to torch it myself." Bert grinned. Aaron looked at Grace. She took his elbow and guided him to his car. "We're only fools in turn. As long as we're together, we'll make out." She reminded him that he had family at home. Aaron left, but Grace did not go into the house to box the very few valuables. Instead, she went back to the studio and tried to work up some drawings for a rear addition, all the while walking through the main house in her mind's eye, mentally collecting wedding photos, her mother's jade, Bert's naturalization papers, insurance documents, and as many LPs as they could box. Two hours later, the wind suddenly shifted and then died for good. Bert sat outside half the night until the last fire truck went home.

Grace drifted out.

"What a pig head I am, to make us stay. For what?" She handed him a beer.

"But you would have left if I had."

She shrugged, the way winners on a bad day shrugged.

Where the stovepipe shot out of the roof there was a gap. The hole in the join was large enough, and the downpour steady enough, that the rain seemed to enter the house as filament.

Bert threw down a pot, he wedged cardboard to calm shaking windows, he took stock: frozen juice, tinned oysters, crackers, chocolate bars, eggs, a fifty-pound sack of rice, flashlights, batteries, kerosene lamps, four and a half cords of seasoned wood, one trusty woodstove. They warmed their house by this airtight stove (there was no central heating), harvesting eucalyptus from their own land. Bert could even bake biscuits in a Dutch oven on top of it. In theory.

"Hungry?" he asked.

In ten years of loving her, Bert could only think of

one time she had not been eager to eat, and that was in her first trimester, and then only after having driven up the coast for the better part of the morning. Her appetite and her eagerness to feed it were reasons why Bert chose Grace, and not some other woman.

She looked up more or less in his direction and shook her head, no, thank you.

Bert pretended to let it go, trying hard to remember if she ate breakfast, what she had for lunch, whether or not coffee counted as food. He wasn't used to doing what came so naturally to her—coaxing conversation. Grace could cook up talk the way she would whomp up a savory meal, using a bit of this and a half of that, food he himself wouldn't have the energy to throw out. And because the meal was conjured from what was at hand, she would never repeat it, no matter how delicious. Not be able to, not want to, any more than Getz would repeat a riff or play a song the same way twice.

Once he brought home some Chinatown tripe and Grace took a long look at it, as if she had questions about touching it. She wanted to *eat* it, of this he was sure. Bert leaned close and slid his hand into the back pocket of her jeans. He stared at the tripe, too. "We could order in a pizza." She stared at the honeycomb lining and wondered how it might look sprayed gold. By the time Bert was out of the shower, the tripe was on the table with whole black mushrooms and slivers of chicken, garlic, ginger, and scallions. She waited until he sat down before igniting it with brandy and a pinch of white sugar. Bert nodded with enthusiasm. It was nothing like how his mother had made it. But good.

"What? You didn't write it down?"

If Bert had learned one thing about Grace, it was the futility of writing things down. Where was the challenge, the delight, in doing what had already been done? To occupation, she also applied this philosophy, working for a time as a production manager for a major clothing line, a job involving monthly trips to the factory in Hong Kong; then as a fund-raiser for a big-five disease; and now, as a landscape architect, a job for which she actually had a relevant degree. Each time, Grace walked away from more money and another promotion, toward unknown promise and the seduction of discovering something new about herself. She took major turns so often that after ten years her mother still feigned surprise to see Bert at family gatherings, her arched brow never failing to convey the astonishment, *Néih juhng·haih douh?* What, you still here? And Bert would answer with a hug, lifting the grinning mother off her feet.

The wind kicked up and scraped an oak branch against the side of the house. Bert appeared in a Hawaiian shirt and very dark glasses. He slicked a hand over his hair. Grace looked up. A trace of a smile. It was a start.

He stuck a penlight in his mouth and thumbed through his collection, Ella, Billie, B.B. King. He paused at Ray Charles. When a song's first-class, everyone wants to sing it. Ellington, Gershwin, Cole Porter—they set a standard. Ella and Ray each recorded one by Porter, "Ev'ry Time We Say Good-bye." Bert loved Ella for the breeze in her voice, Ella, who, when she sang with Louis Armstrong, picked up the tempo and raised the key a sweet fifth. Taking on the same lyrics, Ray had to add a long *Ohhh* before he could even get started. No offense to Cole Porter, but Ray's *Ohhh* made the song. When Bert felt lonely, when he needed a lift, it was Billie, or B.B. King, or Ray he wanted to hear. These were the voices that had drifted up the alley into his room his first months on Alice Street, housewarming from faceless neighbors. Window wide open, chin on the sill, butt on the floor, Bert learned his English—bar by breathless bar.

Ray tonight. Only Ray.

Brother Ray accompanied himself on the piano, his own best sideman, setting a pace so slow, Bert wondered how he would ever be able to get through the song. It's a Ray thing, this slow tempo. How slow was he? Ray could be so slow, the story goes, that you could walk in on a session just as he's giving the downbeat, *One,* cross the floor, take off your coat, unpack your instrument, and still have time to sit down before he said

Two. Ray spun out a spare line of resignation, before the bass and drums eased in. It's an old story: he's waiting, she'll waltz home whenever. Even more than the pace, Bert loved where Ray inflected his lyrics—not on the expected *you*, but on the intoxicating, habit-forming *hooked.*

Bert reeled. He had half a mind to grab his sax. Sit right in.

She had not even looked at the smoked oysters he had set down at her side. Perhaps he should have taken them out of the tin. Bert rubbed his nose, cold and damp. And hers—she who sat as far as possible from the woodstove and still be in the same room? He shut connecting doors; he threw out lap blankets. Hot food was in order. Yet besides brunch, Bert only knew how to cook one thing, and that was rice. Hot, steaming rice.

For the first two months he lived on Alice Street, he made rice in a white tin pot set on a hot plate and ate it with *dauh·fuh.* Cooked it in the pot, ate it out of the pot. An indeterminate amount of rice, an unspecified amount of water, and if the rice burned, salt the lid to take away the smell. Once a week he poached an egg in a depression in the steaming rice. His "village uncle" finally got him a job as a busboy at an all-day teahouse. He was a tall eleven.

Grace hadn't budged.

When Bert opened the door of the woodstove, the fire roared out its appetite. He fed it fat logs. He washed the rice in frigid water and set the pot on the stove. In a flurry of efficiency, he cracked two eggs into the only clean container he could find, a cut-crystal dessert bowl. And without thinking, he took a pair of chopsticks and whipped the eggs into a froth, adding water, salt, pepper, a bit of desiccated green onion, a bit of soy, giving himself up to a method born not of spoons and measures but of witnessing that which had never been explained—a rhythm in the wrist and back. When the rice was ready to cover, Bert eased the crystal bowl on top, very pleased that he had dirtied just one pot, just one bowl. He jerked the crystal out again—was he crazy? Surely it would crack. A wedding present to boot. And from her side of the family. Hell, it was leaded and a quarter of an inch thick. He would take the chance.

The eggs steamed.

Grace lifted her nose. Interest. Just a bit.

How his mother had timed the cooking, how she divined the exact moment between runny soup and dried-out soufflé was knowledge known only to her and the eggs. Twice he reached for the lid, twice he hesitated. He decided against the watch and instead sat down to read the paper, in much the same way that Grace had been reading her book. He cleared his mind and waited for some signal.

His mother's muse was frugality: an egg and a bit of water stretched for the whole family. When he ate steamed eggs, when he smelled them, when he saw them, when he so much as imagined them, he would be reunited with this other family, the ones who stayed behind, the ones who pushed him out of his boyhood toward a better world. A better world without one's family Bert could not understand, but at eleven, he had put his trust in his mother's will. A little blue S of a vein would rise on her temple, definition in an unlit corner of the room. She would turn her attention from another task and lift the lid with confidence.

Bert stood. The custard had set.

Their first spring in the house. A knock on the door.

Grace was coloring the drawings for the landscape design of the new downtown plaza. A fountain, she was going to persuade the clients. Water soothes, water is music, water brings birds, birds provide more music. Tranquillity at half the price. A second knock. Grace poked her head out of the French doors of the lean-to, where the house extended an arm in welcome. Two young boys stood facing the screened front door, the golden one at the top of the stairs, the older one at the bottom.

She walked out as if she had been expecting them all her life. "Hi."

The boys turned in surprise at the direction of her approach.

She fanned herself with her hand. "Thirsty?"

The older brother looked her up and down. "You speak English?"

"I'll speak any language you want."

"You don't know Dutch. You know Dutch?"

Grace warmed to the clarity in his eyes. "I know some Flemish."

"That's Dutch. Say something. Say, 'This is my son.'"

"Dit is mijn zoon."

"Dang."

Her smile was benign. *"Een mooie dag voor een wandeling."*

He studied her for a bit and then nodded. *"Ja."*

The younger brother was still waiting, looking intently into the dark and cool house, more like through the house, to some greater beyond. The older brother explained, "There didn't used to be a house here."

She smiled. "Does my house look new?" She tried to see the house through his eyes. It was a restorer's dream, undercode and neglected.

"Years and years ago, when our daddy was a boy, there didn't use to be a house here." He turned and pointed. "See the path? It goes straight through your house to our house on the back side of the hill."

Grace walked up to the younger boy. She had an urge to rumple his hair. She went around to the far side of the veranda and looked out. The hill sloped up to two mature oaks. There was no path.

"How you know Dutch, lady?"

"I knew a boy from Brussels once."

"A boy like us?"

"A little older."

The younger brother hadn't moved.

"He can talk, lady. Doesn't want to. Been almost two years." The boy squared his shoulders, then slumped again.

The younger one did not fidget, yet his eyes were lively.

Grace thought of the singer named Ray whose music Bert played daily, and how as a child this Ray slowly went blind after watching his little brother drown in the tub. Glaucoma was the official story, a pressure on the eyeballs.

"You Indonesian?"

"Chinese."

"Can you say some Chinese?"

Grace crossed over to the screen door and opened it wide, framing the younger boy under the arch of her arm.

"Chéng yàhp·leih." Please, come in.

They did. They came every day, up the stairs, through the house, and out the back. Grace nudged living-room furniture to clear a path. She inched the kitchen table toward the back door and set on it a plate of classic cookies she taught herself to make, mounding the pile high so a handful would not be missed. Client meetings and construction visits were rearranged for the mornings. The afternoon became her favorite part of the day, the rap on the door, them walking through.

Grace sang. She put on Bert's tapes and when she moved around the studio, she swayed. She drew trees in pots, trees in the ground, quick, sure lines that defined plane trees and poplars and liquidambar, naturalizing—on paper—a perfect shady grove. This was her signature, the positive suggestion of the specific. Why use a dozen strokes when four or five would do? The trick was knowing which strokes were the right ones. This information came to her in a direct bypass of the brain, like many of her good ideas, and over time this facility fed the fiction that she could do just about anything. Overcome just about any hardship.

Almost dusk one afternoon, and no knock on the door. For weeks they had been coming, and like the summer sun, they had given the expectation that they would be around for a while.

Grace walked out to the road. From there she turned and looked back at their house and sighted a distant point that might be a marker on the boys' path. On the spine of the hill were the two oaks, under which she and Bert had often picnicked, made carefree love. She hiked up to the crest and looked over the back side. Cows in the distance, black and brown.

That night, Grace found Bert in the wood shop. "Bert," she said. "I want to have a child."

It would take them seven years. Seven years during which she read all the right books; seven years of seeing one doctor and then his brother, of taking all the tests and allowing many of the interventions, and then finally doing not a thing; seven years during which Bert added on a room, matched interior and exterior details, sandwiched insulation, hung double glaze, and nailed down hardwood. Seven long years during which their hope atrophied to a thread, and neither could imagine an impotence other than the one at hand.

If. When Grace wanted to punish herself she asked the questions that began, If.

If Bert had stayed home that morning, as he'd originally intended? If she had thought to break a lifetime habit of showering upon waking and instead had switched to evenings, when he was home? If she hadn't insisted on moving deep into the country so far from the mother and sisters who were more than eager to help? If she had thought to bring the bassinet right into the bathroom where she could peek at will from behind the shower curtain? If she had finished five minutes sooner? Four? One? If Lucy were alive today, Bert would have been greeted by her face of delight from where she would be sitting on the floor, stuffing every block and ball and finger and toe into the laboratory that was her mouth.

Throughout these long summer months, Bert had been diligent in avoiding certain words. Blame was one. He managed to say instead, "These things happen." And, "Don't worry, Grace, we can have another." Grace whipped around and nearly slapped him.

Last night, before the rains came, she was lying on the floor near the woodstove. Spread out in front of her were picture books, small books for small hands, books illustrated in tropical colors, books full of whimsy, books so new that when she opened them they cracked. One by one she had taken them down, read them, then packed them into a cardboard box. In these tales, the animals talked, and children were abandoned to their own instincts. Other tales were set in elastic villages where no one grew old, where one could sit under trees that sprouted magic thorns—*your every wish.*

"Did you know that the ocean is more than twelve thousand feet deep in places?"

Fifteen. Bert counted fifteen words. More than she had said in a month.

"No light down there, Bert. Plants don't grow."

Another eight.

"It's so dark at the bottom of the ocean, the fish come

with their own high beams, sometimes with strings of colored lights. Look Bert—pilot fish. Lantern fish. Wonderlamp. A floating summer party."

She opened a pop-up book. A paper safari lunged out at her. She could almost hear the roar.

"Why, Bert? Why did we have to fall in love with her?"

Bert held the newspaper as steadily as he could.

She packed that book and another. And another.

After a while Bert walked over and offered her a hand up.

She leaned forward. "Bert, tell me, so I don't forget."

His hand extended farther than his voice. "Come to bed. It's late."

"Five months, you haven't said a word. Where do you bury it, Bert, your grief? Out there under that stupid tree?"

Rain falling through miles of sky makes no noise. Only when it hits does it sound. Bert leaned out the window, moving his eyes as if trying to follow the descent of a single drop of water.

He lit two lamps and set them on the low table at his end of the studio so the light would not disturb her sleeping. Moving among his own double shadows, he rummaged through the drawer of his drafting table, then through the drawer of his desk, and then through hers, collecting pencils and pens and brushes, anything loglike with which to construct a house. He sorted out the stubbies for half-walls where a window might go. For the front door he used an erasing shield—a metal template punched out with basic geometric shapes, a circle, a square, a triangle, a teardrop, a fat line. When the house was finished, Bert set a votive inside and imagined he could see through this door the stars and the moon.

He straightened up and rubbed the back of his neck. Behind him, Grace slept fitfully in a blue down bag.

Words, she wanted. The back room addition, the young cedar—these were his words. Oh, so loud, each time he passed. Aaron had said when a child is born, a tree is planted; a pine for a boy and a cedar for a girl. When two people marry, a branch from each tree is cut and the two are woven together to form a ring. Bert thought it was a fine tradition, but why stop at one tree? He had envisioned a grove, a tree for every month of Lucy's first years, so that over time, the landscape would be transformed by his declaration. Couldn't Grace hear any of that?

His last four batteries.

Words. Here were words, the most gorgeous language he knew. Getz, Lady Day, Ella, B.B. King, and the singer who lost his father, brother, and mother before he found his manhood, the singer who lost his sight and found his calling, this singer whose mother had the wisdom to name Ray.

The batteries ran out. She slept.

This couldn't last forever. Not his Grace.

Bert walked out on the veranda. Rain angled into his shirt. He should have swept the roof last month. He would have to climb up there in the morning and un-plug the drains.

Six months. They had known each other six months when they bought this house. That first night they had made love in there, right where she was sleeping, among the boxes, on the floor, the French doors thrown open, the light of the moon articulating every blade of grass. So it seemed. Afterward, she rolled off him and mapped his hairless body. He asked, almost shyly, "What do you like?" Meaning, where would lines be drawn? She an-swered, "I like it all. With you, I like it all. Anytime, any-where, anything. You, Bert. You, you, you."

She moaned, half out of her bag, her clothes in dis-array, hairs wet on her face and in her mouth. Bert went in. He took time to straighten everything. As he smoothed her dress over her belly, he saw the scar. He was startled to find that the incision hadn't healed, not quite understanding that the ropy line was as healed as it ever would be. He traced the scar from end to end, and again, as if revisiting the site of an accident.

With nothing else to measure against, he used the

spread of his hand. Space enough for a newborn's head, her narrow shoulders. He turned his palm up. Lucy had lain there, her head had been cupped, there.

Grace woke suddenly to the realization that they were in great danger. Her mouth was so dry, her tongue almost stuck to the roof of it. All this moisture, her mouth so dry.

The room was orderly. Not a thing out of place. A dense quiet. She had never understood just how much order disturbed her, or how much she was a part of it. She yanked her legs back into the sleeping bag. Grace, the fearless.

Nothing moved in the studio.

How long had she sat here? How long had she slept? How many heartbeats does it take to forgive oneself? And how many more for something out of one's control?

Dust floated down. Grace lifted her eyes.

To find him she just followed the wail.

Somewhere under the starless night, he was standing in the drizzle. From the direction of the lament, she guessed he was alongside the cedar, ankle deep in mud, blowing the most wretched notes on his saxophone.

After a pause, he began again to reshape the anthem.

She came out only far enough to hear. The cold bit into her.

He was playing so slowly, it took her a few bars to recognize the song—*America, the Beautiful.* Ray would be proud. Taking a long breath in between, Bert worked from piece to piece in his unhurried pace. *A Sunbonnet Blue and a Yellow Straw Hat. Night and Day. Some Other Spring. I'm Just a Lucky So and So.*

Early on, when it became evident that Bert couldn't sing a note, she had bought him this saxophone—a tenor, like Getz played. From the way Bert took it out of the case, she knew she had done the right thing. He had taken lessons on and off, practiced on the back side of the hill, playing to the cows so long, his lips were numb to kissing. She told herself he would play for her when he was ready. She thought that he might be decent, knew he had it in him, but never had she imagined he would sound like this: reverent.

Bert turned and saw her. His clothes were so saturated they hung down in points. Still, his shoulders were square. Oh, he was gorgeous.

"I see you finally decided to get up."

She tried to match the lightness in his tone. "Hard to sleep with all this racket."

He fingered the keys. "Two days shy of eight months."

"That's right."

"Think she can hear me?"

"As if you were whispering in her ear."

He nodded.

She was about to go in.

"You sticking around for the second set?"

"Yes, Bert Ching. Yes, I am."

He stood like a heron. After some time, he put the reed back in his mouth and began something, oh so new.

Thirty Yards

Two men watched Christine play tennis, though she saw only the one. Before the afternoon was over, this one had her phone number. The other, the other slipped away.

The other slipped away while Christine played. He slipped away and appeared on her front porch. George Yee stood in a sliver of sun and waited for someone to let him in. He studied the doormat, the brass around the doorbell, the curve and hang of the knocker. He counted every cymbidium on the porch and noted their various colors. He counted the steps that led him to this door, this moment. He touched nothing. Sunday, the lunar new year, 1965. Leaves whirled down the sidewalk but the Changs' porch was swept clean. George peered in the window. He rang again. Both parents came to the door.

For Christine's father, George Yee delivered a letter of introduction from his uncle, who was to Mr. Chang no more than a name; for her mother, he brought a bag of Chinatown tangerines. Mr. Chang took out his glasses and read the letter twice. Mrs. Chang felt foolish accepting such abundant fruit from this stranger. But because he claimed kinship to a childhood friend of her husband's, and because in her own home she assumed her family had sanctuary, Mrs. Chang overcame her apprehension. She gave the stranger tea.

When Christine returned at dusk, George was still there, Mr. Chang had exhausted his reminiscences of George's putative uncle, and Mrs. Chang's cooking schedule had been completely compromised. The teenager slipped her racket into a wooden press and set the wing nuts, breathless not from the game, but from an encounter with a certain new young man. She pulled her sweater over her head, exposing a brief line of flesh, and stood in a love-struck stupor. She barely acknowledged George as she shook his hand. She excused herself, but not before assuring her mother that she would be out soon to help with dinner.

Dinner.

The word hung in the air for awkward seconds after the girl breezed off.

"Well," said Mr. Chang. "I imagine you already have plans, it being the new year."

"No." George smiled. "No plans."

"Well, then." Mr. Chang looked to his wife for help. She was equally at a loss for words. "Well, then," he said again, pushing himself up to a stand. "You must eat with us." And Mrs. Chang resigned herself to entertaining this obscure man for a few hours more.

Christine locked herself in the bathroom and studied her attitude in the mirror, trying to remember the set of her face when Deiter Varzi said hello. How long had he been watching her, how many days? He had appeared in the beginning of the second set and asked permission to watch, if it wouldn't distract. She thought yes, it would, but said *please,* and was amazingly cool when he thanked her by name. He knew her name! Christine lifted her face to the shower's thousand kisses. Deiter Varzi! Deiter Varzi's every movement was traded from the lips of senior girls named Penny and Colleen, girls with tennis courts in their backyards, who lined their eyes and sprayed their blond and auburn bouffants stiff, who labored over every imagined imperfection in their faces while whispering *Deiter, Deiter,* about the one who was new, was older, was exotic—this Deiter now possessed Christine's phone number. Mosswood 4-5009. Christine closed her eyes and slid soapy hands, as if they belonged to someone else, over high firm breasts, down past the French curve of her belly.

"Christine?" George Yee insisted, offering her the winter melon soup Mrs. Chang had just served him. Here he was with Christine, the girl of blunt-cut hair, who wore semisheer blouses and stuck an occasional daisy in the spine of her book, he was *here,* in her home, at her table. The hem of the tablecloth that grazed her lap grazed his.

Conrad, her older brother, looked at George and thought: *turkey.* Christine looked at him and thought: *virgin.* She accepted the soup with reluctance.

Her father did his duty. "Fourteen years we lived here, now we are all citizens. Took the oath the same day Mr. Kennedy became president. Nineteen sixty-one, January 20th." An auspicious day for citizenship, though had he been naturalized in time, Mr. Chang would have voted for Nixon. "A stain on America, his murder. Full daylight, and the Secret Service failed to protect him. In this country, it's easier to be killed than to be naturalized. Anyone with twenty dollars can get a gun. I can. Even you." He turned to George.

Mrs. Chang sipped her soup. "Where do you live in San Francisco, George?"

"Yes," he nodded, purposely mistaking the syntax of her question. "I will move here soon. I like Oakland."

"Warmer here," Mr. Chang added. "No fog. Not so crowded."

George nodded. America was vast. A man could lose himself in this country.

"And your family, George?" Mrs. Chang persisted.

"I came alone."

He was awfully pleased with himself, for an adult.

Christine was more than ready to dismiss him, but then he grinned at her with such raw assumption, as if they had shared some unspeakable intimacy. Christine stood. She excused herself to serve the rest of dinner.

Crab was their traditional New Year's feast, two fat crabs finished with black bean garlic sauce, flanked by mounds of shiny green *gai lan,* and all the rice their stomachs could hold. Half the pleasure was in the anticipation—*two* crabs! If that man had called the week before, or even yesterday, her mother could have bought another. Four claws for five people! She rooted around in the drawers for another nutcracker and found none. She and Conrad would have to share. She slammed the drawer. Who just drops in on New Year's Day?

Christine shook herself. If she wasn't careful she'd blame George for everything that had ever gone wrong or would go wrong until she died, from the occasional bad timing of her serves to Deiter Varzi maybe not calling her at all. Maybe he was at this very moment sitting at Hy's drive-in with Colleen, sharing a malted and a good laugh at the sophomore's expense.

Mrs. Chang spun the lazy Susan until the crabs faced George. "Tell me, George, what kind of work did you find here?"

"I...am student. All day, full-time."

"Oh? Good. Very good. What are you studying?"

George nodded confidently. "Maybe dentist, maybe doctor."

Mr. Chang perked up. "Christine, too! She also wants to be a doctor."

"Dad, I do not."

Conrad broke his claw in two and drew out the pink flesh.

"Sings her flute like the silver voice of God."

"Dad—"

"Her tennis, better than Conrad. Backhand mean like anything. Wears her own letter, right there on the sweater. You play?"

George nodded, but no one believed him for a minute.

Her mother passed her nutcracker to Christine. "Where do you go to school, George?"

"One more year at San Francisco State. Then, Berkeley." He named the most prestigious school he could think of.

Christine cracked her meaty claw in several places. Twenty-seven years old and just getting his undergraduate degree. What had he been doing in Hong Kong all this time?

George caught her staring at him.

"Better hurry, Mr. Yee. You're almost too old to get into medical school."

"Christine!"

"Doesn't matter how smart you are. And, you should stay in San Francisco."

"—Christine! Apologize!"

"I meant no disrespect, Dad," she said, wiping the

sauce from her fingers, "but you and I both know Berkeley doesn't have a medical school."

The evening was ostensibly over but somehow managed to last another hour. Because George didn't have the grace to leave, Mr. Chang resigned himself to showing him the carp pond that he and Conrad had dug and landscaped. For his rheumatism, the father poured a brandy fortified with assorted roots, tree bark, mistletoe, and red wolfberries. They sat in silence and George stared not at the fish of good fortune but at Christine illuminated in her window, playing with her hair as she made halfhearted attempts to study.

On his way out, George cornered Mrs. Chang in the kitchen and asked permission to take the girl to the movies.

"What?" the mother asked. "Pardon me?" Let Christine go out with *this* man, about whom she still knew next to nothing? Mrs. Chang dried her hands on her apron and did what she had wanted to do from the very beginning—she ushered George Yee to the door.

"My Christine is too young to date."

George flinched, unaccustomed to being denied. He shifted his weight. Mrs. Chang's hand went instinctively to her throat.

Since the birth of her daughter, Mrs. Chang had been unshakable in her fear that Christine would die an early and violent death. That no one believed the story did not prevent it from being repeated by the sisters— Christine's maternal aunts—of how, when she was born, Mrs. Chang saw the shadow of death's lips brush her baby's own in an obscene and audible kiss, and how the baby's insatiable eyes followed the ghost assassin as he slid out of her bedroom like a wayward bead of mercury. For years Mrs. Chang hounded her husband with visions of a demon so unlike them, who would take Christine for his bride and would possess her so completely, they would then be left to wonder had she ever been theirs at all. For the first year of Christine's life, Mrs. Chang refused to go to America. In that land of strange men, anyone could be the assassin of her dreams. Ever preoccupied with her daughter's welfare, she forgot that the first line of attack is to get rid of the guard, and this one oversight cost her her life. A week after George's visit: she wasn't looking, she wasn't careful. She left the hospital after her shift and a swerving car struck her dead.

If nothing else, Mrs. Chang's death spared her from having to bear witness to her own prophecy, and perhaps even helped undermine the power of her dreams. But these thoughts did not occur to her husband, who could not begin to fathom any consolation for the violence and seeming randomness of her death.

In a village with a high birth rate for girls, in a culture that placed more value on its swine than on these same girls, George Yee's mother, a simple woman, gained uncommon prominence for delivering a son of pure physical perfection. *An extraordinary precious,* everyone whispered, *you are a thousand times blessed.* Mrs. Yee pulled him to her breast and wept. She scrutinized his playmates for suitability, keeping the girls at arm's length, girls who fought for the chance to wipe his bottom and deliver an innocent kiss. Like Mrs. Chang, Mrs. Yee also had a dream at the birth of her child—that her son would die of his love for a woman, a woman who would remake his soul, a woman so formidable already her powers had made themselves known, though she herself was not yet born. The dream persisted and without deviation, and in this way Mrs. Yee knew it to be true. To save her son, she sent him away while still a youth, sent him from his country, from her, from her visions. In so doing, she forfeited her happiness and comfort in old age, and lost not only her dear heart but his potential bride—a woman who, had she not been a demon, would have become, as custom dictated, her loyal servant.

Two mothers, two dreams.

If the power of dreams compounds over time and with the attention that the dreamers keep them alive, then it would follow that Mrs. Yee's premonition (which preceded Mrs. Chang's by the number of years between the births of their two children—twelve) would be the more persuasive of the two: George Yee would be consumed by his love of an emerging woman.

Christine bathed her mother. She dressed her all in white—funereal white—white underclothes, white slip, white dress, white jacket with elbow-length sleeves, and she cried, she cried to see her mother's broken body. One witness said Mrs. Chang had turned her head suddenly, as if responding to an urgent cry from someone she knew. Another said she turned only as the car was bearing down, the steady horn a clear signal that things were horribly out of control. But all agreed it happened fast, yet each one marveled that Mrs. Chang had the extreme fortitude to lash out at the oncoming car with her folded umbrella.

Mr. Chang fell into a mood. He worked, he shopped. Conrad washed the dishes. Christine cooked and cleaned, and on Sundays ironed her father's chalk white shirts, shirts whose lives she had not yet learned to extend by turning their collars and cuffs. The men lived through her artless meals and tried not to lose appetite. In the evenings, they retired to their respective rooms and said not a word.

No one gave George Yee another thought. Not when he had slipped in uninvited to sit in the back of the chapel, not when he had given a most inappropriate smile, first, in the middle of the service, and again, when the girl stood up to view her mother one last time, and finally as he left, and with such snap that all that could be seen of him was the dazzling white lining of his jacket.

Christine's tennis game fizzled until she was almost bumped from varsity. This the coach was willing but reluctant to do, for the focus the game gave the girl in this period of grieving. But before he could sit her down, Christine pulled herself together. She poured her uncertainties directly onto the felted ball, even as it spun away from her. Her serves attained a certain hostility, and her opponents tried not to take it personally. When they made attempts to connect to her long drives, they misjudged both the speed and the spin with which a ball could be set in motion by a girl so porcelain. Confident of her power and placement, Christine would almost turn away before a volley was completed. Once she did turn a hair too soon, and despite vindication, she warned herself not to do that again.

A tournament in an outlying city. Christine bounced the ball before tossing it high into the air. At the top of her swing, on her toes, arm gathering speed, she saw George Yee behind her opponent, outside the fence. She faltered. Her serve just cleared the net, but she failed to return the ball. Love–15. She concentrated on her routine. Bounce twice. Toss. Point. Swing. At the crest of her serve, George hooked his fingers through the chain-link fence. Her return was called out. Love–30. She toed up and bounced the ball. Toed up again. Fault.

The second serve hit the service court at a sharp angle. Christine rushed the net and drove the ball clear to the fence at George's face. Coach sat up. Game point. Walking back to serve, Christine wondered which was worse, George staring her down as he was now, or him standing at her back, which he would be doing at the end of the game, when she and her opponent changed sides.

He called her father that night. He gushed about Mrs. Chang, said he would always remember her many kindnesses, and when could he come pay his respects? He asked about Christine but not about Conrad. Mr. Chang reminded him that they were still in mourning.

George called again the next day, in the afternoon, when Mr. Chang was at work.

"Christine," he began. "We can go to San Francisco on Saturday. We can have *dím·sām*. We can go boating, walk in the park. We will go in my car." Christine declined, citing the same excuse she heard used by her father.

The next day the school secretary came into her biology class—a family friend had an urgent message from her father. Christine looked up from her frog, her scalpel. George stood at the door. She drew the knife down the frog's belly. "He's no friend." After George had been escorted out of the building, she went to the office to phone her father, who only confirmed her deductions.

The bus home from the dentist meandered through

Chinatown and Christine's heart beat harder each time she saw a woman her mother's age. One wore a blue sweater with a chain at the neck. Her mother had such a sweater, which now sat in the top of Christine's own drawer. When the woman got off the bus, Christine fought the urge to follow her, to invite her to tea. She stared after her for so long, she nearly missed her stop. Only as the bus pulled away did she even glimpse the beige jacket, the plaid madras: George, sitting in the back, smiling his singular smile with such confidence that he didn't have to look at her.

The next hundred times George Yee called, Christine didn't pretend to be polite. She hung up. In the roily silence that always followed, she heard only the word that began his every sentence. *We. We. We.*

Since his wife's death, Mr. Chang renewed his devotion to numbers. He extracted percentages, totaled columns, assessed differences, until he arrived at some economic distillation, equations for which he felt such confidence, he recorded them in India ink. His retreat into the closure of balance sheets was so successful that by the time he returned home, he was ever surprised that his wife was not there to greet him, that he would no longer receive her touch.

Conrad rode his motorcycle increasingly alone, forsaking the leather jacket but fortunately not the helmet, so that when he hit loose gravel on Skyline Boulevard, his skull and face were spared. While recovering he took up smoking, and his father revealed, to Conrad's surprise, that he had once smoked but had given it up at his wife's request. In the evenings, the two men could be found lighting up on the front porch, so as not to foul what each still thought of as Mrs. Chang's house.

In the absence of mother, and then of family, Christine sought out resilience. She banged into things that would not give—walls and rules. It fell to her father to tear down her arguments for autonomy, equity, bralessness. What he did was to lay out twenty dollars on the kitchen table and tell her to buy some new clothes. On the question of dating, he was out of his depth.

Deiter Varzi wasn't anything a person could put a finger on, half this, a quarter that, an ounce or two of some other, none of which was Chinese.

Mr. Chang scraped the dishes. "He's too old for you."

"Three years." The girl washed and rinsed. "You had plans for George and he's practically thirty. What kind of accounting is that?" Should she tell him that George had been calling her, following her? When she had told Conrad, he said, "Are you sure?"

"George?" her father asked. "George Yee? George is not for you."

Mr. Chang took his Chinese daily into the living room.

Christine sprawled on the couch. Her mother used to sit on this couch with her, let the girl rest her head in her lap, occasionally stroke her face.

"I just want to be friends. Get to know him a little before he has to leave."

"He's not like us."

"He's very close to his family. He writes—" She caught herself.

"He writes what?"

"He writes to his mother every week."

"Why he writes to her?"

"She lives in Germany."

Mr. Chang flapped his newspaper. "Mother in Germany. Boy and father here. Home in Persia. What kind of family is that?"

Persia. For her Persia existed in the distant past, in Scheherazade and Schahriah, where a king could take a bride at night and kill her at morning in atonement for another woman's sins; where a woman was inspired to free herself by wit alone, by controlling the one thing she could control—her story.

"I think about Mother every day. I'd write her if I could."

"His mother is not dead. Her place is here. With him. With his father."

Mr. Chang got up to go bathe.

He filled the tub and soaked. He trimmed his nails.

What did he really know about suitability? The men he thought appropriate, Christine would not even consider for an afternoon of tennis. And the girl lacked wifely qualities, she lacked subtlety. There were ways a woman could acquiesce with grace—how could his wife die before teaching her something so fundamental? He shook his head. The demon suitor. No, he couldn't watch over her with his wife's diligence; there just weren't enough hours in the day.

She was sitting at her desk, her work surface a warren of paper—opened texts in German, biology, American history, trigonometry; reports in various stages of beginning. Instead of a pencil she held two ball bearings, something like a gift from Conrad. She rolled these balls in her hand, partly out of nerves, partly to strengthen her grip. Mr. Chang was hypnotized by the music of metal gliding over metal, by the wavelike motion of her fingers.

"First I want to meet him."

She sat up. "Yes? I can go?" She ran over but stopped short of throwing her arms around his neck.

Her young man, her fair-haired, olive skin that never burns, green-eyed, half Persian, quarter German, a dash of English and Dutch, Deiter Varzi picked her up in his father's two-door, five-on-the-floor, ferried-across-the-ocean Alfa Romeo. Red, from bumper to bumper.

Mr. Chang looked at the tiny sports car, looked long and hard at Deiter Varzi. The young man stood there and took it. The father tried to see him through his wife's eyes. Was this aggregate man the assassin of her dreams? He wasn't surprised he was asking himself those same questions of his wife's that for fifteen years he had poohed and pahed and dismissed as a mother's failure to come to terms with her own limitations to protect.

Deiter leaned over the piano to look at photographs of the family. In them, the children framed the carefree mother in more innocent times.

Not this one, Mr. Chang thought. *He's not the one.*

"Be home at eleven."

When they returned at ten minutes to, they parked several doors past her house. Because the three-hour film played only in San Francisco, and because Christine had to be home by eleven, they had to leave *Doctor Zhivago* at intermission. The teenagers had gone expecting the romance of the decade, had gone expecting to see Zhivago make love to Lara, and saw instead, in that first half, a man of unconscionable appetite—the older, powerful Komarovsky—seduce, whore, and humiliate the young girl and her mother, for which Lara repaid him with a public bullet. It was Komarovsky whom Christine took home with her, Komarovsky who haunted, with his complex passions and dark insatiabilities.

An unlit sedan coasted to a stop several cars behind the Alfa. George Yee rotated the handle on the parking brake before pulling it up, so as to make no sound.

Deiter walked Christine to the door. Her chest rose. Something clanked to the ground. Deiter started.

"It's just Conrad, in the garage." She hoped the moment was not lost.

Deiter regained himself. "Next Saturday?" he asked. She nodded. He leaned toward her. She kissed him.

In her mailbox the next day, she found a movie stub folded in a note: "Our first date, my Queen."

Queen! She looked at the envelope. No return address, no stamp. She glanced up and down the street, assuming it was Deiter, looking for Deiter.

When Conrad went out the next night with his friends, and while her father was yet again late at the office, Christine wasted no time in calling her friend.

"Your Queen is alone," she said. In his hesitation she wondered how she had erred.

"Christine?"

"Yes."

"Would you like me to come over?"

"Yes, please."

She was calm, cool, and collected—until she heard his car. When she couldn't wait any longer for him to ring, she threw open the door. Deiter was bent over, intent, picking leaves from a plant in the side garden. Some old urge was being satisfied. "Mint," he said, barely looking up. "We make tea from it."

Christine pulled ropes of mint out by their hairy roots.

She put on the kettle and got out her mother's china cups, one a pale green with pale pink roses, the other ringed with violets.

Deiter stemmed the mint and rinsed it. "My mother made this for us, *Pfefferminze Tee,* with lots of honey."

Christine pulled an enormous tin from the cupboard. "Honey," she said. The can was new. She applied the can opener and promptly slit her thumb lifting the lid. Honey mixed with blood. She sucked her finger. Deiter drew her over to the faucet and held her thumb under cold water.

"Don't touch me in the house." A lame joke but he was kind enough to laugh.

He dried her fingers and applied the Band-Aid she pulled from a drawer. She might never wash her hand again.

She stepped back. She poured tea.

"Don't touch you at all, or just not with the hands?"

She smiled without looking at him. Oh, she had questions. What was his home like? How old was their city? What was it like to have parents from two different countries? Which language did they speak at home?

"Do you miss your mother?"

"I think my sisters miss our father more. They're ten and twelve, still babies. I was ready to start university last fall. Yes, I miss her. I'm very fortunate, aren't I?"

He gauged the lines of her shoulders, the lines of her

neck, noted that even while standing still she somehow gave the impression of being in motion. "You remind me of her."

"That's not possible."

"Your concentration, the tennis. Your grip. Is it you who plays the piano?" he asked.

"Conrad. He can do anything. Does your mother play?"

"On the concert stage. That's why she's in Germany."

She got down a tin of almond cookies. "Conrad says boys don't like strong women."

"Some don't. My father is such a man. Twenty-three years together and he still hasn't figured out that her independence is what he loves best about our mother."

"And you?" She passed the cookies. "Do you like strong women?"

"I have my father's instincts and my mother's sensibilities. It is truly an inconvenient place to find myself."

She blew ripples across the surface of her tea. "We have this dance in the fall, on Sadie Hawkins Day. The girls invite the boys."

Deiter crossed his ankles. "Who did you ask?"

"No one. There wasn't anyone worth the battle with my parents."

He took a good look at her. She suddenly seemed younger than he had thought. "How many boys have you gone out with?"

"One."

"One in addition to me?"

"Just one."

He shook his head. Laughed. "They don't ask you out, either?"

"I didn't say that."

He took another cookie. "You don't like to just have fun?"

"I make them nervous. They don't look me in the eye."

"Maybe they're shy."

"I'd like to have that shy feeling, too. That heart-pounding feeling."

"You don't get lonely staying home by yourself?"

"Spending an evening with someone you have nothing in common with—that's lonely."

"How can you know if you don't spend time with them?"

"I spend time with them—in class, at lunch, after school. Girls don't get to choose who asks us, we only get to say yes or no." She wondered if she had the luxury of saying no because she was invited. Would she be so content to stay home if no one called?

"It's scary for the boys, too. We have to take the risk, to ask the girl. Will she be merciful and say yes, or will she be a destroyer of hope?"

"Do you want a girl to go out with you when she's not interested?"

"Sure. I think, an evening with me and surely she'll change her mind."

She laughed. "Does it work?"

"Yes! Sure. Most of the time."

Between them were hundreds of years of arranged marriages; of bound, mangled feet; of chadors covering every inch of a woman, from her most sacred thoughts right down to the red, red earth.

Her cup tinkled against the saucer. He caught it before she realized she was spilling.

He hadn't shaved since morning. Would his skin feel rough? Would she like it?

He set her cup down and put a hand on the counter on either side of her hips. Along with mint and honey, she caught a trace of almond. He bent and kissed her behind the ear.

"Is this all right?" he asked, surprising even himself.

"Yes."

She wondered how slowly he would go, how far he could, without his hands.

A few nights later, the chance she was waiting for, once again alone. Never had she been so grateful for tax season and her father having to return to the office after dinner, for Conrad ever excluding her from his plans, as older siblings did with impunity. She was already dialing out when her brother doubled back and pulled up under the breakfast room window. She leaned out, holding the phone below the windowsill.

"You going to be all right?"

"Of course. The Shumakers are home." She pointed. The neighbors' curtain dropped closed.

Conrad mulled something over. "You want to come?"

He never invited her, especially to join his friends. "To tear up the dirt? No, thanks."

He pulled off his helmet. "I told Dad I would stay home."

"Dad should be more worried about you. I didn't crash on my motorcycle. I don't smoke." Conrad wasn't smiling. Any moment now he would turn off the engine.

"Look, I'll call—"

"—Rose?"

"Yes. Well, Rose doesn't drive, but I'll call someone." Conrad put his helmet back on. "Lock the—"

"—Already did."

He pivoted the bike around his outstretched leg.

"You're not bad, for an older brother."

"You are a pain in the butt."

She waited until he turned the corner before dialing out. Deiter said, "Thirty minutes."

She scurried around the house, tidying up. She ran outside to pick some mint, leaving the front door open. When she turned around, her nose buried in the herb, she saw first his shoes, then his pant legs, the khaki jacket, the long barrel of the rifle in the crook of George Yee's arm.

A gun. Shit. She didn't say that. Her eyes swept both sides of the street, seeking out any sign of life, and found none. A gun. Oh, Mommy, help.

"George," she said.

Don't look at the rifle. Keep talking. Calm voice. But what to say? Nice to see you? Is that a new gun? A rifle—was he serious? Was she safer outside, or in? In, the door was solid oak. In. She took the stairs one at a time. Head up. Way up. All the time in the world.

"It's unfortunate my father isn't here to receive you." No use pretending she wasn't alone. Surely he knew.

George didn't budge, but he did smile.

She gained the porch. Four more steps and she'd be inside. He blocked her. She dropped the mint. He bent to pick it up. She passed him, a fist apart. *In.*

He straightened up and handed her the bouquet. She looked him right in the eye and began to close the door. No smile, no more.

George leaned toward her. His words slid in on a whisper. "Don't touch me in the house."

She bolted the door. She checked the back door. Called the police. Misdialed three times, made the same mistake three times. She stood in the dark, in the center of the house, touching nothing. Even her clothes felt like invasion. Her hands swelled. She was hot. Open a window. Don't. George came. George left. Deiter came. The police came. Deiter made her tea. Conrad returned. Con returned.

Deiter let Conrad in. The officer looked up.

"Con, it's OK. I'm OK. He came with a gun. George came with a gun."

Conrad took it all in. He looked at Deiter. Looked at the officer.

"He was waiting for you to leave."

Her brother smarted. She didn't mean for him to feel blame, just the opposite. Conrad stepped between his sister and her boyfriend and thanked him in a way that suggested Deiter could go. But the officer wanted to question everyone. He wanted them to sit. Conrad stood. Deiter stood.

The officer eyed Conrad's beat-up leather jacket, his scabbed palms and knuckles, and suggested that perhaps it was he that George wanted. "Maybe you two are in a gang?"

Conrad laughed. "George is a loner. He's after *her*. He's been following her."

"I thought you didn't believe me."

"I believed you."

On the dining table was a pile of unopened letters, no return address. She waited for his response, she would gauge her danger by his response.

Conrad now added a large flat box. "It was on the porch."

Christine made no move to open it. The policeman took out a pocketknife and slit the tape. Beneath layers of tissues were a veiled and heavily beaded headdress (a leaden thing), a jacket, a floor-length skirt, all cut from a red silk brocade embroidered with gold.

Christine paled.

Conrad stuffed the dress back and closed the box up. "A bride's outfit."

Deiter put a hand on her shoulder. "Can you arrest him?"

"It's not against the law to send letters and gifts—"

"What about the *gun?*" Conrad interrupted.

"He didn't threaten her. If he has a permit, and the rifle wasn't concealed—"

"What, does he have to shoot her—"

"That's the law, boy." The officer flipped his notebook.

Each backed off and tried to remind himself of their common purpose.

Had George slipped in while she was picking mint? He'd been in their house before—even invited—and had walked through every room, had used their bathroom, fingered her still damp towels. Rubbed where she had rubbed.

"He's there," Christine whispered.

"What?" The officer unbuckled his holster. He peeked through the blinds. "Where?"

"Outside, on the street, in his car, behind a bush. You don't see him, then—there he is. He's been there all along." Her voice was frighteningly flat.

Her father got home in time to hear what the police could do: not much.

"George," he said, still holding his briefcase. "George is crazy. For him, this is a game."

"He's going to hurt me, isn't he, Daddy?"

The officer pocketed his notes. He looked ineffective and felt it. "There's the restraining order. You'd have to go to court. He'd be there, too." He turned to Mr. Chang, father to father. "It's hell when they're obsessive."

Obsessive. Is that what it was? Obsessive?

Christine walked Deiter to the door, not knowing what she was going to say. She said, "I can't see you anymore." She described George down to the mole on his cheek, the down slope of his shoulders. She said, "Be careful." And, "I'm sorry." And, "He knows who you are." Then she tried not to think less of Deiter, or of his feeling for her, because he did not protest.

Thirty yards.

Thirty yards was about as far as she could swim without feeling as if she were drowning. Thirty yards was how far she could drive a tennis ball before it bounced, though it would be out of bounds. It was how far her voice would carry, unless she screamed. That's what the judge said, thirty yards. No closer. Christine knew what thirty yards truly signified. At a practice range, and for handguns, thirty yards was the average distance between the shooter and his target. With a rifle, thirty yards would be a challenge only if the shooter didn't take aim.

Four people sat in an overheated room: the judge, who barely looked up when she walked in; her lawyer—a linebacker in college, a decent man, a third-time father-to-be. The fourth person in this room not much larger than her bedroom was George Yee, deliriously happy, unrepresented George. This was the closest he had been to her in weeks.

The venetian blinds were sticky with dust. Christine longed to open the window, to stand in air that moved, to expand the limits of this room. How could any decree of note possibly emanate from a room so close?

Her father had said, "The lawyer will do all the work. Next Tuesday, 10 A.M. Don't be late." She was sitting on the floor against the doorjamb of his bedroom, bending a paper clip back and forth, working it apart, piece by piece. "Daddy, please come with me."

Mr. Chang looked up. His child was wedged in the frame, spilling out, her bony wrists protruding beyond faded pajamas. He smiled at her, the first time he had smiled in weeks. At that moment, if he had asked her to walk on fire, she would have given it a try. "Conrad will take you," he said kindly. Conrad. Conrad wouldn't be able to sit still without smoking a pack, which the judge surely would not allow.

"It's OK, Dad," she said. "I can do it."

The judge huddled with her lawyer. He asked her no questions. He asked no questions of George. Outside his window were a couple of bottlebrush trees. She counted the red blossoms. If she ran out of blossoms, she could start on the leaves.

Twenty minutes later the judge signed with authority. He slapped the restraining order on the desk.

"Violate this, young man, and you go straight to jail."

George smiled. More than a smile—it was a triumph. He just had to keep his distance. Thirty yards, it said. No closer.

Christine fingered the order. She examined the front and back. Just a piece of paper.

Night came, but not sleep, not deep sleep. She would wake at the merest sigh, broken out in hives, throat constricted, her heart some wild thing, and then be alert until dawn, teased by the proximate sleep of her father and brother. For company she had her thoughts, her nightmares—all of him—where he was, what he would do, say, want. Thoughts of George filled her until there was room for not much else, not food, not tennis, not sleep, especially not sleep. If her mother were in the next room, she would slip in and sit down at her bedside, and her mother would cover her with her own robe from the foot of the bed. Christine would ask, *Mommy, why me? Is it the way I look? Is it because he can't have me that he wants me all the more? Is it really me he wants, or is it the idea of me? What is the idea of me? Who am I yet? What did I ever do? And, Mommy, why is he always smiling?*

The prudent immigrant kept to the letter of the law. He continued to follow the girl—to hound her, watch her, record her every movement in a cheap notebook bound with metal, his girl, *his,* thinner by the day—and always he was diligent in maintaining his distance of thirty yards. No farther.

When Mr. Chang drove Christine to school, George was ever ready and waiting, thirty yards down the street. He stayed thirty yards behind them all the way to school, turning when they turned, stopping when they stopped, and Christine took note of her father's nerve. On the days Conrad did not go to the university, he drove her on the back of his motorcycle.

One bright morning Conrad pulled out of the driveway and waved to George. Christine was appalled. When George fell in behind them, Conrad spun right around, whizzed past George, and squeezed between the two lanes, right on through the yellow light.

"How fast can this thing go?"

"Last week I did eighty-five on the MacArthur."

"Jeez." She hadn't even gone that fast in a car.

"Hold on." She felt his stomach tense.

When he banked, she banked. The blacktop came up at her in a demonstration of centrifugal force. George ate dust, and the siblings sped for the false sense of power. Conrad detoured by Skyline Boulevard and at each corner she wondered if this was the site of his accident. She pressed her cheek into his back and let him take all the wind. When they coasted into the school yard, her thighs were jelly.

"I *never, ever* want to go that fast again." She hobbled off.

Conrad rolled his bike up on his kickstand. "That's because *you* weren't driving."

"Uh-huh," she said, but she got his meaning.

He scanned the yard in his casually comprehensive way. Satisfied that she was safe, he said, "Later."

Christine pulled off her helmet and shook her hair loose. She didn't know why she was staring across the street—just a yapping chained-up dog and an old willow tree. But neither could she look away. Then George Yee emerged from the shadows, arms hanging loose. Right at that moment she hated him. She hated George for his every intrusion, his relentlessness, his assumptions, his theft of her privacy. Mostly she hated him for what he brought out in her—real fear, a hardness, more metal that she ever wanted to know she could possess. She could go to trig and history and lunch and on to her afternoon classes and two hours on the courts, and George would stand out there all day long. Sun, sleet, rain, snow.

How far would she have to move to feel carefree? Fresno? Idaho? Mongolia? This she now knew, long before decades of frustrating statistics would confirm her suspicions—thirty yards, thirty thousand miles—if George Yee wanted to kill her, he would.

The bell rang. The second bell rang. George stared at her. She could stare, too. He had no idea. She grabbed her books. She grabbed her tennis racket. Move even one muscle. Blink, sucker.

A hot, summery spring day, a bird-singing day, a heart-skipping, racket-twirling, short skirt, legs-free day. Buds, birth, renewal, hope. She left school with Rose, with laughing girlfriends. She herself laughed, she tried. Rose smiled and brushed wayward hairs from Chris's face and Christine nearly cried. Talk stopped, the girls fell back. A shot. What sounded like a shot, followed by the buzz of confusion. A second shot. Kids screamed and scattered. George at the curb, fifty, sixty yards away, savoring his effect.

Not today, oh no, not today. Who was she kidding? No day would be good. Where's Conrad, which class, where? She wanted to look. Don't look. Christine worked the problem. By the time the police arrived, George would have shot her. If Con were to run out now, George would kill them both.

She dropped her books, her purse.

George was startled at her declaration. He expected her to run. He wanted to see her run. She didn't run. She advanced. No! "Christine!"

Stay on course. Do not cry out. She would have to get close enough to spit. Oh god. Forty yards.

"Stop!"

Thirty yards. George danced in place.

Twenty-five.

"Stop, Christine!"

Fifteen yards. Don't cry. Not yet.

"Stop! Christine, stop!" His arm came up, the gun a rude extension of his delicate hand.

"No, George. *You* stop. Get away from me. Leave me alone."

George stepped back. He fell right off the curb.

Her bile came up but he heard it as a snicker.

He shot her once.

The slug tore clean through her neck. She faltered, regained her footing, put a hand to her wound, and brought it back sticky with blood. She rushed the last yards and slammed him with her racket. She hit him as hard as she could, a two-fisted backhand. The wood press caught him square in the cheek. She hit him! Oh, no. She could hardly breathe. The next bullet hit the trees. She cracked his elbow, he dropped his gun. She hoisted the racket over her head and nearly whacked him again. They bled on each other. They fell to their knees.

Christine painted the house. Her father and her doctor and even Coach thought it would be restorative. She began with the bathroom, starting early, while the day was cool. By noon she tired. Always, she had the thirst.

Deiter visited. Her father rotated and misted his wife's orchids. Conrad adjusted the timing on his father's car

while Deiter held the timing light. Christine soaked her
brushes in turpentine. Then she and Deiter sat on the
front porch in full view of every car that drove by and
slowed down. He had visited her at the hospital and on
the day she came home, and never mentioned the senior
Colleen, or his waking with his fingers in her auburn
hair.

He was going to Germany with his father, where his
parents would try again. At the end of summer, he
would begin university in London. They sat on the
porch and sipped their colas, and Christine asked about
his mother, measuring each word like gold. It hurt to
talk, to swallow. Her throat was purplish brown and
swollen and Deiter didn't stare, he didn't look away.
They sat on the porch and she spun out, in her mind,
that afternoon's events. By the time the police came, she
had broken George's elbow, she had broken his jaw, she
may have blinded him, one retina was detached. As he
had on the other visits, Deiter waited until she had spent
herself. After a while she said, "I almost killed him."

He took her paint-speckled hands in his, held them,
turned them, as if this were the image of her he wanted
to carry away. They sat on the porch. They talked. He
talked. She leaned into him. When he said good-bye
she didn't ask him to write, and he didn't offer to.

Rudy's Two Wives

Despite the cold, Cecilia sat in her car until she saw Rudy enter the coffee shop. His clothes were mussed, but she doubted that he had slept in them. He did have that dry-mouth look. She finished her cigarette. When the traffic cleared, she buttoned her coat and pushed into the wind.

Rudy stood when she entered. If he still had the habit of wearing hats, he would be holding it now. She liked the time when men wore hats.

He had called her. No more than a week would go by before he called; she just had to wait. But it was she who had suggested this place, halfway between their homes, no longer at ease with him coming to the house. Now she wished she had come in first and had chosen her place, so she wouldn't be the one sitting with her back to the door.

"Ga·fĕ?"

"Mh·gòi." Thank you.

He ordered her coffee. That's how it was between people in their generation, and no one thought anything of it. For himself he ordered a strawberry shake. She suppressed a smile. A kid's drink. Had he hinted of an ulcer sometime back?

Ulcers aside, he was looking fine—no stoop, still a full head of black hair at fifty-eight. She had been salt-and-pepper for ten years, but that wasn't why people assumed she was older. No, it was her self-assurance. That and Rudy's consultation of, and deference to, her. Even when they were in college, people had made that assumption, when in fact Rudy was her senior by two years. Married thirty-three years, divorced one, now here they were in a cavernous coffee shop nowhere near Chinatown, where the owners (themselves recently arrived from some Chinese outback) made fresh donuts at six and three, and lamb with yogurt on Fridays.

Their drinks arrived. She stirred two lumps of sugar into her coffee.

"Did I snore?"

"Yes."

"You never said."

"Nothing to say. I snore, too."

"I never noticed."

She crossed her ankles.

"She's been sleeping in the guest room. She said my snoring keeps her awake." Cecilia plopped in two more sugar cubes. "Then she said the mattress on the guest bed was too soft and gave her a backache."

She was Li Li, Rudy's new young wife, and so often a topic of conversation he didn't need to refer to her by name.

"So. She moved back into the bedroom with you?"

"Well, no. I mean, yes, she moved back in, but then I moved to the guest room. Really, it was thoughtless of me not to give her the bed from the start. After all, she just had a baby, and I was the one snoring. Did it ever bother you?"

"Not at all." On the contrary. Hearing him breathe when she woke at night reassured her of his continuing viability, of hers.

Cecilia lit a cigarette, even though she hated people who smoked at the table. But she didn't think she would be able to get through the next hour without something to settle her down.

"You smoke now?"

Rudy sucked the milk shake through the straw. The icy drink made him wince. He should sip.

"So, you've been sleeping in the guest room—?"

"—Three months."

That would be August, about six months after the baby was born.

"You try sleeping on your side?" A nudge was all it took to roll him over.

"That's what the doctor suggested! The snoring has

really improved, even Li Li said so. But now she says the baby makes her so tired that she sleeps even more lightly."

Soon it wouldn't take much more than a sigh to wake this dolly.

"So which room do you meet in, when you want to—"

Rudy broke down. "She says it hurts her. Not that I hurt her, but doing it hurts her."

Now Li Li was refusing Rudy, and he's taking it hard. Good. But how dare that child reject her Rudy?

"She should see a doctor. Could be something not right about the birth. Could be complications."

"Complications?"

"It's probably just a cyst."

"A cyst? You think so?"

A cyst would be too good for that husband stealer.

"Is that serious, a cyst?"

"Not if it's benign. Just a growth." But she knew some growths could get pretty big. Big like a grapefruit. Big like a baby.

"Good thing we're married and she gets her insurance through my job."

She should just get up and leave. Right now.

Rudy played with the straw, oblivious to her suffering.

He had insisted she take the house and half of their savings. That was the finite price of his guilt. He walked away with a young wife, a new life, an heir. She got assets and an empty bed. Her girlfriends wanted her to make him suffer, because if such a decent, devoted man like Rudy could—well, they didn't even want to finish that sentence. But they needn't have been concerned. Cecilia understood suffering. If she raged at him, sure he would feel guilty. But at home, safe in the pillow of his bride, he would be only too relieved to be free of her. And she would be stuck with all that hard feeling. No, there was nothing to do but be nice, so nice he'd torture himself day and night for having ever given her up, and for that *hèung·há pòh* who couldn't even open a bank account by herself.

In the meantime Cecilia made herself comfortable. With the house (a twenty-year roof with nineteen years left), the savings, and her own income, she would make out fine. Yet she continued to be prudent in her management of funds. Then, too, as a systems analyst, she made almost as much as he. With his share of the savings, Rudy barely had enough for a down payment on a decent house, a house with which Li Li was quite content until she saw the house Rudy left behind. He also put money down on a car for her. Brand-new. When had they ever bought brand-new? Thirty-two-year-old Li Li with her bad teeth and a Miss Chinatown body. Those teeth would cost a bundle, but Rudy had dental that covered half. Good thing, because that degree of hers was useless in this country. She would have to start over, get certified, before anyone would hire her to teach any sort of mathematics. In the meantime she could sell something. That's what immigrants did, sell things. Surely that *sai yú* had untapped talents for sales.

"Her brother arrives next week. Her sisters will follow with their mother after the school year."

A family of three mushrooms to seven.

"We're converting the garage. Of course, they'll be living with us. They're family."

She winced.

Cecilia wondered if the point of this urgent meeting was not the sleeping arrangements but whether he was desperate enough to want to borrow money from her. And would it give her more pleasure to accommodate him, or to deny? She never thought she would live to regret the familiarity they had with one another.

Look at him. His face still soft, even as he approached sixty. Lines, yes, a puffiness, yes, but the countenance of a child. For a Chinese, he was a big man, big and broad, with bright upturned eyes. In thirty-some years, Cecilia had never heard him say an unkind word. Nothing pleased Rudy more than to be useful, to be of help, her Rudy of the genuine smile. Of course Li Li saw these qualities, too, how could she not? Cecilia's mother had cautioned her to keep looking, saying, he's not quite a man yet, implying that Rudy might never be. Sure, he was honest. Hardworking. Dependable. Kind. All to be valued. But he had little spine, her mother implied. That was all right, Cecilia had spine to spare. She had liked his lack of calculation, his total obliviousness to craft. He walked in on her twentieth birthday looking like purity. She would have him, and told him so, even before the idea was a dividing cell in his brain.

They never had children. She didn't mind, and he said he didn't either. She looked out for him, and he blossomed. Her girlfriends spoke of him with admiration, spoke to her with envy. Her girlfriends marveled that for more than three decades Cecilia and Rudy ate lunch together every day and never lacked for anything to say. They envied her ability to be content and more with uncomplicated Rudy. Cecilia wasn't fooled; she knew Rudy wouldn't do for them. For all their complaining about their own husbands' shortcomings, they also fitted with their partners, and if they did not somehow relish the struggle of their daily lives, they lacked the daring to live any other way.

"Were you unhappy with me?" Right away she wished she hadn't spoken.

"No, never. Never."

"Bored?"

"Not a minute. You're the smartest person I know. Except for Weyland." Weyland was the head of engineering.

She hadn't meant bored in that way, that talking way.

Rudy hung his head.

He and that princess didn't talk. His increased appetite for Cecilia's conversation told her so. At first it didn't matter, he and Miss Chinatown discussed other topics,

topics in which that *gùng·jyú* was very articulate. Then, too, she had vocabulary enough to praise—his handsomeness, his cleverness, his passion. Rudy wasn't more passionate than the next man, but that *yéh jyū* telling him he was made it so. Her words gave him a strength and daring and fearlessness. Who could deny such a woman?

At night, alone in the bed they had shared all their adult lives, the hardness Cecilia always feared she might possess surfaced, and to her increasing alarm, she found her heart running along those same paths worn down by her late mother: why give that cheating *móuh yīu·gwāt* his freedom? How come all these years, he doesn't give you a baby and the minute he looks at her, she's big with child? You sure it's his? Keep the husband, keep the baby (his baby is your baby), let him put that *chip·sih* in an apartment. Why give up your rights as first wife?

Partly for the need to spite her mother (even though she was dead); partly because they weren't in Canton anymore (only one wife at a time!); partly because some part of her really didn't believe Rudy would go through with the divorce (when had he ever made a serious decision without her complete participation?)—for these reasons and more, Cecilia did not so much agree to the divorce but *dared* it to happen. Then, too, there was the screaming dazzle of the unborn, who, had he been born in China, would have had a 51 percent chance of being a boy, and had indeed become a boy—what argument could she possibly construct against a *son?*

Oh, so much Li Li understood. If she had to marry for profit, she would at least choose someone nice, and they didn't come any nicer than Rudy. If Cecilia had fought for him, she could have saved him all this agony. In her arrogance, she had dismissed Li Li's plot as marriage/ miscarriage/green card/divorce. Well, it turned out she was wrong about the marriage, wrong about the miscarriage (8 lbs., 5 oz.), and now she feared she would be wrong about the divorce, too. Li Li wouldn't give Rudy a divorce until all her family were here and green-carded, not until her sisters were through school and themselves settled, and her brother firmly established. Cecilia hoped the brother was a proud man, that he had his sister's ambition, her filial devotion.

"Once a month she lets me come to her bed."

Her bed. Once a month. Cecilia almost felt sorry for him. Once a month was a pittance compared to what he told her they had been up to. Such daring, such imagination, such stamina, and for a man his age. How could a woman like sex so much? Rudy, at fifty-eight, a father with a continuing line. Of course that woman was having trouble sleeping. How could she sleep? She had lain down with a man she did not love and she bore his child. Could she love the child? Oh, Cecilia, how American. For Li Li, this was no more than an arranged marriage (albeit one which she arranged herself). If ever they were to meet, she would slap that *tàuh·gèh* red in the face.

"Cecilia?"

"Yes?"

"Can we leave? Go to the house?"

Foolish to think things could be different if she just made them meet in a public place. She knew his needs, not excessive, not demanding, but regular. She had needs, too. To be held and warmed as only one could be warmed by another person. To be talked to in a voice so quiet there was no room for pretense.

The last time they made love (and there had been a number of times since the divorce), he announced his intentions so abruptly that he knocked over his tea. That night Rudy had walked in and right away noticed the back door was binding and a struggle for her to open. In the time it took for him to plane the door, she had the opportunity to notice that his hair needed cutting. Like teenagers sneaking out a bedroom window, they thrilled to the boldness of this intimacy, knowing that Li Li missed nothing—where at that hour could a decent man get a legitimate haircut? Afterward, what could Cecilia do but pull out of the fridge the *ngàuh·nàhm* she had prepared especially for him (the beef practically melted on the tongue) but was until that moment unsure she would offer?

It was after this very satisfying supper (Rudy ate three bowls of rice), and just as they began to section their grapefruits, that he suddenly stood and took her by the hand and swept her up with his desire, which so overwhelmed the both of them, they never quite made it to the bedroom. Afterward, he could barely look at her, his every new gesture having only betrayed the frankness of the intimacies he had shared with his new wife. He had taken Cecilia's hand and made her touch him, excite him, and while she didn't find it unpleasant, it was still a shock. What happened to the shy and tender man who had been her husband?

Cecilia set her gloves and handbag on the table. The waitress caught Rudy's signal and nodded.

A wind blew in. *Fùng!* was more like it. *Fùng!* The click of heels. The waitress stopped in midpour.

Li Li tramped in, babe in arms.

Rudy stood.

The baby bucked. Li Li tightened her grip on his thigh. Oh, he looked so much like his father that Cecilia couldn't help but smile.

"You!"

Cecilia turned. Li Li slapped her hard. Heads turned. The baby screamed, inciting all of Cecilia's finer instincts.

Rudy held out his arms. "Li Li, give me the baby."

Baby Rudy strained toward his father. Li Li renewed her grip. Her eyes teared. Her breasts leaked milk. The baby's face puffed and reddened.

Cecilia tasted blood.

"Li Li, give me the baby."

When had he learned such authority?

The young mother teetered between confusion and sheepishness, between anger and the shame of having actually struck someone. Not just someone, an elder.

Rudy lifted his son out of his mother's grip, held him close, and kissed and kissed him. He rocked and swayed. Cries became sniffles. He turned Li Li by the shoulder and led her out, pushing into the night.

The wind shifted and blew their coats open. Newsprint kited through the air. Even as she was being led away, Li Li twisted around and held Cecilia in her sights. Cecilia dared a glance. Li Li was pretty, but not so pretty, not so curvaceous, not anymore. And no more self-assured than Cecilia was. In fact, Li Li was nothing like Cecilia imagined. Rudy had to urge her on, but not before Li Li had taken the baby.

The waitress ran to shut the door. People turned back to Cecilia and lit her with their curiosity.

She dabbed her lip with a hankie, being careful not to get blood on the embroidery. She buttoned her coat, needing every occupation to collect herself. That Li Li Yee knew a thing or two. She knew what was important. Protecting one's family was important. Knowing what in all the world you really wanted. And then, fighting for it. No mystery why Rudy was smitten. No mystery at all. Under other circumstances, Cecilia thought she, too, might have been drawn to her.

Talking in the Dark

Gravel gave way to mossy brick. Claire dragged her fingers along the pickets. A delicate but woody vine wove through the nasturtium, spiraled around the gatepost, and sent all its energy into large star-burst flowers. Clematis, whose showy sepals passed for petals in a flower with no petals; clematis, so voluptuous it was often mistaken for passionflower.

Claire squeezed through the gate. Gangly roses lined both sides of the path that led to a stucco house with a tiled roof and a painted porch. The yard and the house had the dry look of neglect, but she could imagine both in better times. She glanced back down the path toward her car. If she hurried she could still get to chorus before the rehearsal began.

The front door opened.

Russell smiled, clearly happy to see her. "Come in, come in." He opened the door wider, raising a hand to his heart to draw a circle, as he remembered she had taught him to do, and signed the word *please.*

She had never stood next to him before. He was taller than she realized, so vivid, every hesitation, even in the fading light. Yet, he looked right at her eyes, not at her nose, nor her mouth, which was where she usually caught herself staring, at other people's lips, as if to understand better what they were saying.

"I don't drink. Not much." She blushed. What presumption.

"I've cut back myself. But I brought food, in case you hadn't eaten."

She slid her hands into the pockets of her dress. He longed to see these hands in motion, her talking hands.

They passed a living room of exposed beams and hardwood floors. What remained were a love seat, a floor lamp, a leather wingback, and a Belouch runner borrowed from the entry hall. Across the back width of the house, in front of a row of windows, was a dark, almost black, Mexican table with a thick slab top worn smooth from touching, comfortable for ten. But no chairs.

Russell arranged a tray with sliced ham and smoked fish and ripe cheese. He refolded the wrappers and stacked the plastic empties. She could imagine him at the deli, pointing decisively to foods that appealed and then saying quite suddenly—that's enough. Unlike Perry, who reached for everything and was always a little surprised at the sum. Russell pointed to some sparkling water. She opened a bottle for each of them.

"Who lives here, Russell?"

She had never called him by name before. Russell. Nice. That hush in the middle. She once knew a boy named Russell. They were both eleven and he had kissed her impulsively, missing her lips altogether. "Russell," she said to herself.

He was pleased, as if no one had ever paid him that particular compliment before. "The house belongs to a friend."

"Is your friend here?"

"Overnight at his ex-wife's. They're still trying to work things out."

"Kids?"

"Away at college."

What kind of people were they to meet at someone else's home? She should leave. They both should just leave.

On the mantle was a treasure of valentines done in every medium from glitter and lace to charcoal and clay. One was cut from a sheet of brass, cross-slit, the petals rolled back from the center to reveal an inlay of gold leaf—clearly a shop project that had achieved a momentum of its own. *From Rand to Dad. From Shauna to Dad. From Meredith to Mark, all my love.*

"A lot of history on this shelf. But nothing of you."

"I thought you'd be more comfortable here. A restaurant seemed loud." A hotel, presumptuous. They both avoided the word *public*.

"I'm sorry. This is a lovely—" She couldn't say *home*; it was no longer a home.

A large rock dominated the back garden. The neighborhood was defined by these half-buried boulders and no one cleared them out. The house next door used the rock itself as the mother of all cornerstones. Indian Rock, Mortar Rock, historical landmarks whose names recalled a lost era and culture—hunting, gathering, an imperative intimacy with land. Next week, when she longed for some tangible fragment of this evening, she would search out the name of the stone, rhyolite, spit from the bowels of the volcano as fiery boulders. She had to admire people who would build their homes in the path of past destruction.

"It's very peaceful. I'm glad we're here."

"You can deduce any number of things about a person from his home or the way he dresses. But you know doctors. If we relied only on deduction and extrapolation, we would be doing the patient a huge disservice." He poured out olives, offered them.

"In my family inference and intuition were essential to communication."

"This isn't easy for me, either."

"Have there been others?"

His sleeve caught on the wine bottle. She righted it before he was aware of it tipping.

"Just one." Nothing changed in his voice. "We talked a few times. That's all." *She* had talked. *He* had listened.

"That can be a lot, talking."

"It was." He cleared his throat. "I've never done this before, and never with a patient." Technically she was Dr. Dunn's patient. Technically.

"When patients come to you, we're not fine. We're ill, we're hurting, we're anxious. You walk in with your chart and pen, we're practically naked."

"I've said nothing to you I didn't mean."

Yes. His forthrightness was one of the attractive things about him. And then, he seemed such a decent man.

"The first time I saw you, your eyes were closed and you were singing."

She often sang to herself and loudly, a childhood habit. Even now she sometimes forgot that others could hear her. She probably did seem a little odd, but no one had ever found it attractive before.

"I'm in a chorus."

"Was that what you were singing earlier, something from your program?"

"I was singing?"

"Outside. Are you skipping rehearsal tonight?"

"Is that a deduction, doctor?"

He smiled, caught. "What are you performing?"

"A requiem mass, by Fauré. Do you know it?"

The beginning of the *Offertory* gave her particular trouble. The orchestra's plaintive introduction coasted to a stop and left the altos musically naked with an a cappella solo until the tenors mercifully joined in. Supplicant and delivered at a near whisper, this humble plea—full of fear—spun out at a largo crawl and gave voice to innocence. As a group, altos were a stalwart bunch but vocally timid, especially in the limelight. Harmony is what they provided—harmony, texture, a deepening of the tone. To lead with music this transparent, this emotionally bare (no place to hide), required more than they were accustomed to giving, more than they felt confident to give. And yet, they were asked to do just that.

"You could have suggested another evening. I would have changed my plans."

"If there was too much negotiating, I might not have come."

"Why did you?"

Something in his voice made her feel he didn't expect an answer. There was that quality about him, the not pushing. Perry was like that. He had never thrust himself at her. She liked that in a man once.

"I like looking at you. Nothing twitches when you talk." She saw in his face a man who couldn't leave anything out, couldn't lie. But was that the same as not holding back? "I like faces. Faces, hands. My dad had tremendous hands. He could make anything. He worked wood, glass, iron. He even sewed. For a doctor, you have pretty beat-up hands." She pointed to his left where the baby finger curved out awkwardly and back.

"Caught it in a kitchen mixer when I was a child."

"Ouch."

"Ruined my piano career."

"You play the piano?"

"No."

More. She wanted more. "Who are you, Russell?"

"I'll tell you anything you want to know, Claire."

Perry did that, always made her ask.

"Tell me about the line where it says next of kin, and the number of dependents living in your home. Tell me the name of the book you don't want anyone to know you're reading." She traced a circle with her toe. "Name one thing that makes you shiver all over when you hear it."

Elizabeth, Hollis, Sandy, and Moosh, the dog. The book, which book?

"Here's an easy one, tell me the very first thing you put on after you shower."

"My watch. I flunk, don't I?" His mind raced to find the answers to her other questions. Elizabeth also asked the hard question—who are you anymore, Russell?

"You have me at a disadvantage. I don't know anything about you, and you've got my entire history in a manila folder."

"I love my wife. I love my children. I've spent some forty years being a reasonable man and it no longer comes naturally."

He hadn't crossed his arms or flinched, and in that moment he seemed to her awfully brave. *I love my wife.* And how did she feel about Perry? Perry had been gone for thirty-one weeks. Her girls were counting. She dreaded the day they would stop. Between the not knowing and the worry and the anger and the tremendous hurt, she was no longer sure about love. Though if some stranger in a bar were to pose that question to Perry, she could imagine him saying, and without hesitation, *I love my wife. I love my children.*

He was watching her; even as she turned away she could feel his curiosity.

Photos lined the back wall, hand-printed duotones, all of couples. In one, the skyline was so low it seemed to press the lovers to earth. The next pair were separated by an empty street and neither regarded the other. Two in leather kissed under kicked-out windows as the man flattened the woman's wings to the brick. Perry was a photographer, but not portrait. The tundra, the Sahara— these were the stories that called to him.

Russell leaned to get a better angle on the photos. He had eaten many a meal in this room and had never given the pictures more than a passing glance.

Tray in hand, he led her outside to the back patio, where there were stone steps for sitting. Certainly in the

world there were larger rocks, but here, in a neighborhood garden—where few were smaller than a two-car
garage—the rhyolite had a majesty. She leaned against a
citrus tree. He sandwiched ham between some bread
and offered it to her.

Orange scented the air, overpowering the patrician
rose. Claire reached up to snap a twig and her skirt
swung out behind her. He tried to gauge her stride, its
length, whether or not it would match his. She rubbed
the citrus blossoms between her palms. He leaned and
inhaled the perfume, being careful to touch only her
hand.

"I can hardly get on the bridge anymore," she said. "I
don't panic, my heart doesn't pound. It's not a phobia,
but a reluctance. Everything is happening out of order.
Dads are supposed to die first, right? They're usually
older, lead supposedly more stressed lives. Mother was
forty-three. Her sister also died in her forties."

He had noted her birthday because it was just a few
days after Elizabeth's. Same year. Both women had just
turned forty, though Claire seemed not older, but more
pensive. Elizabeth still had not only both parents, but
all four grandparents.

"I know I could go any day, any of us could. Good
health doesn't guarantee long life. Nor does youth. Does
being a doctor make you feel that death is your silent
partner?"

On his birthday, on the birthdays of his wife and

children, Russell gave blood—as a reflection, as thanks-giving. "I also deliver babies and set bones and treat common infections."

He took pride in treating the whole person, in pro-viding a continuity of care over a lifetime. His was a practice of variety and deep satisfaction that served all manner of human suffering, from acute bleeding to nonspecific malaise. Frontline warriors, doctors like him, signed insurance forms on the line that said PRI-MARY CARE.

"Before I started medical school, I visited an internist friend of my mother's. He said that after nearly four decades of practicing, he was still affected by losing a patient and that any doctor who would tell me differ-ently was a liar or a drunk, and if I didn't think I could live with that I had to seriously consider another pro-fession. I stared at the pictures of his wife on his desk, this woman he could not save, and I nodded as if I un-derstood. When I was twenty, I didn't imagine—didn't even think to imagine—what I could not do."

He had been pushing his thumbnail into his forearm, a recent habit, wanting to feel something exquisite, even pain. "Your child at your breast, mine riding my shoulders, a hand laid on the arm of the dying—these moments give life ballast."

He leaned toward her.

She stiffened imperceptibly, as many women did the split second before he inserted the speculum.

He stood and offered his hand. "Come, Claire, let's eat. Then we can go. Nothing has happened."

She turned sideways to him and smoothed her palm over the rough of the rock.

"I wake in the middle of the night and the first thing I think of is you. What you have said, what you might say. Whether or not I'll let you touch me. How it would feel to press myself into you, how we would fit. Then, I can't sleep for hours afterward. The next day I'm a wreck. Tell me if you think nothing has happened."

Two weeks ago, the receptionist slid open her frosted window and announced that Dr. Dunn had an emergency and would probably not return. The next day was Saturday; the good doctor would begin his vacation. Rescheduling for Claire was not just an inconvenience, the receptionist noted. There was no urgency, but an anxiety: the woman wanted the results of her physical. The receptionist squeezed her in with another doctor.

Russell barely looked at her when he came in, but he peered over the top of the chart as he perused her blood count and her bare legs. Urinalysis, liver, kidney, brown hair, steadfast eyes, EKG, salts, normal, normal, normal, no anemia, nervous smile, cholesterol in the low 160s, the resting pulse of an athlete. Each time he had looked up, he found her staring not at the lab sheet, as patients usually did, but directly at him. She was searching there, in his eyes, for truth, for some explanation as to why her heart worked so hard while she slept, yet missed so many beats during the day.

"I wake from a deep sleep and my heart is pounding, all this adrenaline, like I'm in mortal danger. Other times, it feels like my entire electrical system has shut down. I can't even find the impulse to inhale. Then, boom—all the lights come on. Am I having mini heart attacks?"

He scanned her eyes. Focused and alert, not at all glazed.

"What do you do for exercise?"

"I jog, three, four times a week."

He felt along both sides of her neck, checking veins and glands.

"Smoke or drink?"

"No." His hands were warm and sure. "Well, maybe an occasional glass of wine."

"Any family history of heart disease?"

She shook her head.

"Are you under any undue stress? New job? New living situation?"

He got some answer in her hesitation, her averted eyes.

"Did you discuss this with Dr. Dunn?"

"I forgot."

"I can't tell you how often I drive away from the mechanic's only to remember all the other things I had wanted him to check and forgot to mention. Once it was too much play in the brakes." He handed her a paper gown. "Just the sweater. You can leave your bra on. Open the door when you're ready."

All this formality. All this caution. Thank goodness.

He eased down the neck of her gown so deftly she didn't even realize she was helping him. The stethoscope was warm. Her gynecologist did that, too, warmed up her tools. The doctor had freckles on his scalp. He straightened up and handed her the stethoscope.

"Here, listen. A normal heartbeat goes *lub-dub*. Yours has a *ssshhh* in the middle."

He pulled out his pen and drew on the table paper the floppy valve between the left atrium and the left ventricle of the heart. Her father did that, too, drew on paper, but he did it to augment his arguments as a deaf person in a hearing culture.

"Mitral valve prolapse. Go to any party and one or two women will have it. Maybe one man. Occasional palpitations are about as serious as it gets, some breathlessness, maybe some chest pain. Overexertion can exacerbate it. So can stress. It will not increase your chances of heart disease. It will not increase your chances of heart attack." His face was inches away.

She handed back his stethoscope.

"The most difficult thing you have to do is not worry. Can you do that?"

She nodded.

"Is there anything else you'd like to discuss?"

She shook her head.

He finished his notes. At this point he usually shook hands with the patient.

"What kind of work do you do?"

"Do I have to quit my job?"

"I thought you weren't going to worry."

She hadn't been teased since Perry left. "I teach. American Sign Language. Mostly to speaking and hearing freshmen eager for something other than French or Spanish."

"Is someone in your family deaf?"

"My sister. Our parents. My mother voiced a little, though. I learned to sign before I learned to speak."

"Really? And your husband?"

"Hearing and speaking." Though Perry was never a talkative man.

"Your children—?"

"I wanted the girls to be able to communicate with my family. Now they love having a language none of their friends know, and I can't convince them that they're being rude."

A hearing and speaking child in a deaf household. "It must have been hard on you."

She shrugged it off. "I got to watch a lot of TV. TV, radio. Dr. Dunn's idea."

Strong. She had to be; he had seen it often with able children.

"My mother took me to the park every day, not just to

play, but for me to be around speaking people. I'd stand on her lap and shape her lips. *Speak, Momma, speak!* I couldn't understand what bad thing I'd done for them all not to talk to me. Oh, what I put her through."

She had always wondered whether her mother would have been soprano or contralto, whether her father would have been a baritone. Once she had a dream where her sister and her parents not only talked with her and with each other, but they went door-to-door singing Christmas carols. When she woke, she lay very still and let her mind go slack, so she could continue to hear their imagined voices even as they faded.

"What I would have given to have heard my mother laugh."

He usually called his parents once a week, but it had been almost a month since he talked with his mother. He couldn't remember the last time he had heard her laugh.

"It's more involved than talking, isn't it?"

"It's different. Everything comes in through the eyes. You can't sign to someone who isn't looking at you, someone who's reading the paper. Or washing prints in a darkroom."

He hadn't moved from the door. Claire suddenly wished he was the kind of doctor to wear a lab coat.

"Can you show me?"

"Now?"

He nodded.

Her instinct was to sign something light, but her hands had the itch. She signed swiftly, an animated face, the slap of hands, the crinkle of a paper gown. A man packs clothes, some gear, tucks a photo into his breast pocket, loads his car, kisses his family good-bye, drives off. Wife and children wave. Many moons pass.

Her hands drifted to her lap.

"A man goes on a trip, a man because of the hat. He bids his family good-bye. He's gone for some time. Days? Months?"

She nodded. Her hands left damp prints on her gown.

"So, doctor. What happens at the end? Does he come back?"

"I don't believe you got that far in the story."

"You're right. I didn't."

She had been swinging her legs and now stopped.

He had been grateful for the chart in his one hand and the doorknob in the other to anchor him to his resolve not to touch her, not here.

"How do you sign the word *please*?"

Some people could look right at her eyes and still not see her at all, but merely aim their words in her direction. But he was seeing her. She put her hand flat over her heart and rubbed once in a circular motion, without haste.

Please, he copied the gesture, noting that his hand was open, with nothing to hide. "Please," he said. "Will you have coffee with me?"

She quietly reached behind to close up the gap in the back of her gown.

"Talk, was what I was proposing." Russell switched his pen to his other hand. "You're absolutely right. I apologize. What could I have been thinking? Please excuse me."

He was halfway out the door.

"Where?" she asked. "Where would you like to meet?"

They were lit by yard lights in glints. Someone in the neighborhood was playing the saxophone, as someone in his own neighborhood often played the flute on countless other balmy nights, so that over time Russell had come to associate woodwind music with warmth and a languor, with life lived on back porches in full view of neighbors, with Hitchcock's film *Rear Window,* and the open observation of simple, solitary—sometimes painfully lonely—lives, lives that somehow still seemed more engaged than his own.

"Sign language was started in the twelfth century by monks in Spain, as a way to circumvent their vows of silence. *I'm turning in. Dinner's ready. Go with God.* Their need to communicate was so strong that it superseded even sacred vows."

He had been drawn to her concentration, to her ability to create a richer world, and then to give herself up to it. Yet earlier, when she had declared herself, and with such abandon, he had been overwhelmed. He wasn't sure if he was up to that much convergence, even if neither of them were married.

"Helen Keller said that blindness kept her from things, but deafness kept her from people."

Claire watched, amused, as Russell stuck his fingers as firmly as he could into his ears to simulate being in a soundless world.

His heartbeat pulsed in his ear, and he doubted if even this was an experience possible for the deaf. Wonder, then a deep isolation, swept over him. Being lost in space might feel like this. He widened his eyes in the dark, calling on one sense to compensate for the lack of another.

Sunrise, her outspread hands began, her eyes on his. A man squared his shoulders, pulled on his peaked cap, and walked out of his house, carrying his ax. He went some distance, scrutinized the forest, selected a fat tree. Chop, chop, chop. Sweat flew. Chop, chop, chop, chop. The man walked around to the back side, cut a wedge, said, *Timber,* nudged the tree with his finger. The tree fell down.

Sunrise, day two. The man went out with his ax, surveyed the forest, picked out a *skinny* tree. Chop, chop, chop. Back wedge—chop, chop. Said, *Timber,* leaned on the tree. The tree did not budge. The man reapplied himself. Chop, chop, chop, chop. He put his shoulder to the tree, yelled out, *Timber.* The tree stood. He took off

his hat, scratched his head. A second lumberjack saun-
tered over, shook his head, pointed to the skinny tree,
and said, *Excuse me, but that's a deaf tree.* The first lumberjack slapped his forehead.

Before Claire could sign the word *t-i-m-b-e-r,* Russell
was already grinning, grateful and relieved that he had
gotten the joke. The tree, of course, fell down.

Her hands floated down to her side, where they were
obscured by uncut grass.

He was staring at her, going over every inch, starting
and ending with her eyes.

It hadn't occurred to her to wonder what he would
look like naked, only how he might feel pressed against
her, point to point to point; whether he was the sort of
man to fall asleep afterward, or if he was that rarer kind,
one who liked to linger and talk quietly in the dark.

"I'm writing down everything I can remember about
my mother, because I think I've already forgotten half
of it. When I was a kid I loved to watch her hang the
wash. She'd face the back fence and shake out each
piece. *Whap!* And before long there would be a line of
gay flags. At first I whispered—but she couldn't hear
me, so whispering seemed absurd. Whenever she'd
hang the wash, I'd sit on the back steps and after a particularly smart set of flaps I'd sing out, 'I love you, love
you, Momma!' Once, she turned—maybe she had seen
my moving shadow—she turned and waved and smiled,
just as if she'd heard me."

Claire sat on her hands. Russell used to do that, too.

A sprinkler whirled. *Fftt, Fftt, Fftt.*

"She knew. Even I knew. Some fates are so undeniable their odors just hang in the air. I think she hoped the doctor would not dare deliver bad news in front of her child. Fifteen, and I had learned how to spell *oncologist*. But the doctor was an honorable man. He asked if there was anything she wanted to say. 'I'm a young woman' was what she said."

"And your father?"

"A different kind of cancer."

She was at increased risk. Was Dr. Dunn aware? Of course he was, he was the family doctor.

"So, Russell. What kind of doctor are you? Are you the kind who can tell the patient she is going to die, or do you tell the family and let them handle it?"

He took his hands out of his pockets.

"Statistics are nothing more than a compilation of known events, from which we make a statement of probability. But then, there is a vast uncertainty—all of nature—that we cannot control, and barely understand. Why does the fire burn down an entire block but skip Mr. Brown's house? How could one have predicted that the Ethiopian would win the marathon, and barefoot? That one sister would have blue eyes and the other brown? Statistically, you are at higher risk. But, you are not your mother. You are not your father."

"You really believe that?"

"I do. But to be prudent, I would advise regular checkups."

She stared at his hands. Large hands, nails cut straight across, skin smooth, not too veiny, not yet spotted.

After a bit he leaned over and laid his head on her chest to listen with his ear to that steady, sure beat he had heard so recently through metal and rubber tubing. Her heart, about the size of her fist, pushed and pushed against her breast. He could turn his head a few inches and kiss her and she might respond.

"Give me your hand," he said, with quiet authority.

He reached down and pressed her fingers to the break in her ankle. "Here. About as far away from your heart as the blood can go. But feel that pulse. Yours is a strong heart."

His ear to her heart and now his hand on hers. How long had it been since a man had touched her hands, held them, turned them over, kissed them?

"I wonder what your face is like when you sleep, what it's like when you are fully aroused. Whether or not your skin changes color."

"Are you so ardent with your wife?"

She wondered if she could get through the rest of the evening without saying anything else wrong. Had she really believed that she was at liberty just because Perry had left?

Russell walked back to the tray to pour himself some wine. She surprised them both by accepting a glass for herself.

"I've lived with Elizabeth longer than I've lived with anyone else, even my parents." The notion startled her until she added up her years with Perry. "What we talk about is our investments, who will take the car in, the start times of the girls' soccer games. We no longer agree on where to vacation. We don't like the same movies, don't read the same books—which in itself is not a bad thing, but neither of us tells the other about what we're reading." He leaned his forearms on his thighs, feet slightly turned in. "Sometimes I can't help but wonder— if we were to meet today, would she still have me?"

Claire imagined a young Elizabeth radiant with babies. She imagined Elizabeth now at the midpoint of her life, turning pages in bed, searching in her own way for engagement.

Russell had trouble picturing Perry. Was he clean shaven? Heavyset? Younger than he, more fit?

"Where is Perry, Claire? What has happened?"

She leaned into the boulder, seeking its hardness against her back.

"Where is he, where has he gone? You wouldn't be here if he were home."

"No?"

"You're not that kind of woman."

"And, you're not that kind of man?" She laced her

fingers. "Perry went to the Mojave for a two-week shoot. That was in September." It shamed her to even think about it. September. Going on seven months.

"He's missed Thanksgiving, Christmas, New Year's, the girls' birthday. His."

Russell had missed a number of holidays early in his career, making the mistake of putting the needs of his patients ahead of those of his family. Elizabeth met him at the door late one night, declaring for all time that he was either a part of this family or he was not.

Claire stood. It would be easier if she didn't have to look at him. Whenever things were difficult between her and Perry, she wouldn't look at him. If she didn't look at him, she wouldn't be able to hear him. It was a childhood truth and made no sense outside the family.

"He sends a postcard every week to let us know he's well. On the back he draws scenes—some pines, a creek—quiet idylls that give us no clue to his where-abouts, but done with the kind of detail that would eventually make a person blind. The face of the refrigerator is covered with his messages. Is this thoughtful-ness, or some insidious form of control? Some people complain about not getting mail, but what we'd give to pick up the phone and hear his voice."

"You've contacted the police?"

"The police. The police see a man working in his pe-culiar way, they see a domestic situation. Do runaways write home? I flew to Flagstaff, where the first cards were posted, and drove around in widening circles for days. I might even have passed him on the street and didn't recognize him."

Seven months. She must be sick with worry. Did she have enough money?

"For a while, he wrote. Brief, lucid messages. And, he's done this before, but never for more than a few weeks." Art. The muse. She could spit.

"Last month Helmut at the gallery received a carton, could I please come down. In the middle of the conference table was this box, addressed in heavy black marker, no return. I've never seen Perry use a wide marker. Large printing, huge. Inside were rolls of exposed film, zipped in plastic. That's all. No note, no *how are you*."

Why Helmut? Perry had always sent the film straight to the lab. Then she would go by and look at the contact sheets, which he insisted she view upside down. Were the images crisp, was all he wanted to know. This way, when he really needed her, she could still come to the finished prints fresh.

Claire said the film should be sent to the lab.

Helmut concurred. He offered to call Luke, who, Perry had said, did a better job of printing his film than he ever could. Helmut alternatively offered to store the negatives. He then excused himself to take a call, leaving her alone with the gaping box.

Half a year and all Perry had to show for it was ten

rolls of film? Ten rolls could easily have been shot in a single morning. Perhaps he had been waiting, all this time. But, for what? The right moment? The right situation? A confluence of events?

She picked out a random roll. Each large spindle held a dozen 2¼-inch negatives. Perry had touched these spools, had loaded and unloaded them. She wanted to grab the film and run home, dump them onto their bed, summon the girls. It sickened her to think what condition he might be in if he was willing to trust someone else—even Luke—to deliver his hard-earned images, to determine which one or two of his images would say it all.

Then, the real bounty. Every few days, another carton, these with the enormous 8 × 10 negatives, boxed in sets of fifty, sealed in plastic. Hundreds of negatives. Thousands. Negatives as large as letterhead.

"I had to ask myself, where does Perry sleep at night? Under desert stars? And to whom does he whisper the last words of the day? To a new woman? To God?"

Russell's head came up sharply.

"I want the film processed as quickly as possible. Then, I'm afraid of what's on them. Is the work a cry for help? Or is this a parting gift meant to last us a lifetime?"

"He'll come back—"

"—You don't know that."

Why did he say that? Of course he had no way of

knowing. And even if he had, he understood the guidelines. Listen. Be compassionate. No more involvement than an appropriate nod. And, in a grave situation, a slight touch upon leaving.

"A card came last week. A straggler, after three weeks of nothing."

Jamie and Constance had run in, slamming the door open. They propped the card against the toaster and stepped back. It was a panoramic print of the desert taken with a disposable camera and sent naked through the mail. The photo looked like nothing. Nothing at all. Wide, so wide, as far as one could see, just a washed-out yellowy sand. Jamie said, "Look, Momma, there's the sky." Claire leaned close. At the top rim of the photo was a smear of translucent blue, and sandwiched between it and the sand was a hairline red horizon that, in contrast, seemed to shout. She reeled. Was this the picture of utter serenity, or the stillness before some great flood?

"The girls stared at the card for a long time. Then Jamie said, 'Daddy's not coming back.' And they turned to me, daring me—begging me—to deny it."

She paced. "I mind, oh, I mind very much, I especially mind for *them*. I mind that whatever so fascinates him should necessarily exclude us." Was it something she had said? Or didn't say? Something she did? A long series of somethings? Did his kiss good-bye have any hint of finality, anything different, anything at all?

"The other night I walked by the girls' bedroom and heard Constance whisper, 'Daddy's taken a vow of silence and we will, too.' They haven't said a word since. They just sign. It's all I can do to feign indifference. Oh! I just want to shake them hard and scream. There's nothing wrong with them." She cupped her cheek. "And yet, if I were ten and my father had just walked out of my life, I might do the same thing."

"It's a romantic age, ten."

"Yes," she said. Then again, "Yes."

His cadence was perfection. Compassionate and calming. She could well imagine his delivery of the most devastating news.

"I don't expect any more cards. For them, I hope, but for me, I just want, at this point, I want some certainty. Why does he make us work so hard to understand him?"

Russell thought about his contentment in his marriage and practice. He thought about the exasperation that his daughters, even Elizabeth, could invoke, and the wit with which, in the very next moment, they could dispatch to oblivion all the jagged hardness of his day. A smile or a passing touch was all it took.

"Maybe Perry's telling you all he can. Maybe he's answering some urgent call to life."

Late at night, she had returned again and again to this very same possibility. Had hoped for it.

Russell sat on the lawn, straight-backed despite the

ease with which he had delivered his words. She could not imagine him ever walking out on his family. But, did that make him more attractive, or less?

"Have you ever jumped out of an airplane?"

"You mean, with a parachute?"

She nodded.

He shook his head. "Have you?"

"No. Scuba?"

"No."

"Bungee cord jumping?"

He laughed.

"So, Russell. What's the most dangerous thing you've ever done?"

"Oh." A deep inhale. "Euthanasia."

Claire leaned back. She sat right back down. Along with cremation, she and Perry were passionate about death with dignity. No bags or tubes or machines for them. But here in front of her was a man who, by his own hand, had taken it out of the realm of abstraction and philosophy. How big of her to say she was all for it.

"The most recent one was nineteen. Just a boy."

The most recent? How many altogether? Could she ask that?

"Car accident?"

"Lifeguard, swimming alone, on his back. He misjudged his distance from the end of the wall, and how fast he was going. That's the theory. He sustained a concussion and was submerged just a little too long."

"Coma?"

He nodded. "We intubated, hooked him to an IV. Then, tube feeding—three square meals delivered straight to the stomach. Pneumonia. Another pneumonia. Catheterization. Bedsores the size of oranges. For a while, there was hope. After hope, a parent wants something more tangible, a parent wants a miracle. For six months they lived in that boy's room. They signed a DNR. Do not resuscitate. They waited another couple of months, and still got no sign from their god."

"Could you have said no?"

"I hope I can always say no.

"His mother had had a dream. In it, her son was six and came running along the creek bed, splashing water up to his eyebrows. The father had to leave the room." Russell himself seemed to have difficulty continuing. "We threw the switches, we did it together. One for the heart, one for the lungs. Then, she begged him to forgive her."

This Claire knew. It's wrenching to give up hope.

After a while he looked up, as if he'd forgotten that she was there. That they were there. "It's humbling, what we don't know."

What can a person really know, about another, or even about herself? Or what she is capable of doing under extreme circumstances? Could she possibly have anticipated that she and Russell and Perry all could have been capable of such betrayal?

The saxophonist turned in. Having enjoyed his concert, she now savored the silence—which wasn't silence at all. Crickets rubbed their wings. Late-night traffic churned on home. True silence—true silence was unbearable.

"The bells at the Campanile."

"Pardon?"

"You had asked what makes me shiver when I hear it. The bells at the Campanile. They make me stop still."

Yes, the bells in the tower.

The first time Perry undressed her, he dropped to his knees. He said, *Claire, Claire, Claire.* She thought, what a gift, to hear someone she loved actually whisper her name.

"Yes," she said. "Brass moves me strongly, too."

His breath deepened, it slowed and deepened. She knew this sound. It was the sound of someone overcome with strong feeling. Could be desire. Could be fear. She was moved that he'd let her hear.

Claire smiled. She regarded him for a sustained moment before he was aware of the tingling at the base of his spine.

Later, at home in his own bed, Russell wasn't sure if she had also held his hand, or if he had only imagined it.

Later still, he wasn't sure if she had smiled at all, but had only touched him briefly upon leaving.

The Quiet at the
Bottom of the Pool

A moment ago Buck was still holding her.

An hour ago she still knew who she was.

Rosemary Berg lay in her bed for some time. She sat up. Her chenille robe lay on the floor. She could put it on. She did. She crossed the room, letting the belt drag along the floor. The door to the pool was open. She went out.

In summer all the doors that faced the pool were left open, all day long, all night. It was that kind of neighborhood. And as every room of her U-shaped house faced the pool (even the kitchen), every room then had outdoor access, and the whole effect was one of invitation. She and Phil liked the flow of air, of activity, of living, and over the years had added on and nailed over and opened up until a ranch house became this—a haven. Friends swirling drinks said that their house seemed an enormous cabana, as if it were a place of perpetual joy and recreation. As if such a place could exist.

Rosemary sat down on the threshold with her feet dipped in the far edges of the patio lights. From her robe pocket she counted out her nightly allotment of three filter tips, setting two on the ledge next to her. She lit up the third.

She cocked her head. Was that the refrigerator door, was Buck hungry? Or was she so consumed by guilt that every noise sounded like betrayal? A mother has eyes in the back of her head, has radar for high and low pitches, for uncommon silence, for the beginning of screams. A mother hones her instinct for anything that might endanger children. Why then was her hearing deceiving her now? The phone's rotary dial clicked in a pace so slow that it could only be interpreted as stealth. If she turned her head and leaned forward, she could look across the patio to the kitchen window and see him illuminated by the light from the fridge with the wall phone sandwiched to his ear, searching for what in her harvest gold kitchen, as the phone's corkscrew cord limited his paces to four. Yet it was cord enough for her to check a roast, or to glance out to the driveway to see Phil's hand come to rest a little too far down past the doll waist of the secretary she herself had innocently encouraged him to invite. No use looking. Buck had left. Left. Gone. Forever. She heard him go out the door. Semen trickled out. She watched in fascination. No, it was just the ghost of the summer calls. Summers and summers of calls. Whisperings. Giggling. Besides, who could he possibly be phoning at this hour? What could he be saying? Rosemary picked a piece of tobacco from her tongue. Surely she had misheard. How could Buck be talking like that, and having just left her arms? How could she even imagine him doing that? No, what she heard was the voice of her own dark heart.

Rosemary leaned her back against the doorjamb. The pool sweeper snaked over the water's surface, sucking up leaves and spewing out water in radiating arcs.

Buck had been the first to really use the diving board. She liked to watch him dive, nothing special, not like Babette, just a looseness he had about his spine. He had dropped into their lives as if from some exotic corner of the world—was that already seven years ago? He taught Stevie B to dive. He also taught him endurance of manly things, starting with pain and ending with fear, adding that if Stevie B could hold his breath three minutes, he would take him to Florida to swim with dolphins. "When?" she heard Stevie B pant. "When I go, good buddy, when I go." Stevie B still practiced all summer, until one day he said, "Look, Ma," and disappeared. Rosemary was about to dive in in her culottes when he finally emerged at the deep end of the pool, looking like he had just won the 100. Rosemary even enjoyed watching Buck with Babette—in a way.

She used to keep an eye on the children from the

kitchen, where, because of the deep overhang of the roof, the room was always dark and cool. She would boil up some Turkish coffee and sit on the bar stool with her long-handled copper pot, her demitasse, a tower of sugar cubes, and clip articles to send to sisters who had followed their husbands out of state. Invariably she would gaze out the windows at the children. They could hardly be called children now. Stevie B, maybe. Babette was already sixteen. Buck would be heading off to college in a couple of weeks.

One day at the beginning of summer, Rosemary sat and watched Babette swim across the pool, making hardly a ripple. Her heart ached to see the grace of this child. Babette got out and started her dives. Buck and his friend Denny were tanning on the deck. They watched, too, and she saw Buck smile and then lean over to whisper to his friend. Babette warmed up on pikes, then flips, and only hit her stride when she added the twists. Rosemary had not seen her work so hard in a long time, as if the young girl was struggling to find in elusive perfection some other balance altogether.

Buck twisted a rubber band around his hair and alternated dives with her, helping her in the way he knew best, by showing. After a short round, he got out and lay chest down on the warmed brick. Babette continued a punishing series of inwards and got out only when it was evident she had lost her rhythm. Rosemary hated inwards, hated the backward-facing takeoff, always worrying if Babette's head would clear the board on the way down. The young girl dripped over and sat on the far side of the pool with her arms wrapped around her legs. No one thought for a moment that she was done.

Then, without announcement, she climbed back on. The young men opened their eyes. Rosemary wandered back to the door. *Bamm.* Two steps and a spring into the air. At the peak Babette arched, pulled back her hips, and opened her arms wide as if to embrace the entire pool. Sunlight torched the water. The girl pierced its surface to displace her weight in sprays of liquid gold.

Later she lay in the hammock against Buck's V-shaped chest as the two of them slept off the swim. Rosemary looked up from shelling peas. She wondered if her daughter was sexually active, if she and Buck were lovers. Lovers. A ridiculous term for teenagers. A ridiculous term for a balding man and his night school secretary. Amanda. Babette shivered in her sleep. Before Rosemary could even think to get her daughter a sweatshirt, Buck, without opening his eyes, pulled her in closer. Rosemary wondered what her daughter let Buck do to her when they were alone in the house, whether or not he held her afterward.

She was still thinking these things when she got up the next morning to do what she never allowed her children to do—swim alone. Since Phil left, since he moved in with Amanda, Rosemary switched her swims to dawn, no longer being able to sleep through the night.

On Friday mornings, when the children were still overnight at their dad's, Rosemary would do something she and her sisters used to do as girls—swim naked. They'd swim away from the beach, remove their suits, tie them around their necks, and struggle into them before going ashore. She could do that, as a kid.

Now she was naked Thursday nights, too, as soon as it got dark. One Thursday night (was it only two weeks ago?) after her laps and her half hour of treading water to tone her thighs, Rosemary was loath to get out. She flung off her flower petal cap just to feel the water's fingers in her hair. She corkscrewed the length of the pool and back, up and back, one beautiful at-ease twist spiraling into the next. She somersaulted through the water, forward, backward. She dolphined, oh, beautiful back-bend headfirst arcs in the deep end, elongated curves, arms overhead, toes pointed and everything. Phil once said she could have been another Esther Williams. "You have a style," he whispered. "A radiance." That's the way he had talked to her, with real awe and earnestness. They were twenty, the moon was full, the lake was theirs. Rosemary rolled onto her back on the diving platform. She thought Phil would lean over and kiss her, but he dived into the inky lake and headed out for the floats. The bottoms of the buoys were blue and peeling, though this she couldn't see. The white tops she could. Phil waved once and disappeared under the rope. The lake recovered its surface. Rosemary lifted her head; she eased up on her elbows. In the long seconds that passed, she saw the buoys anew in all their power. In the night, the floats and ropes glowed, seemed almost fluorescent. She'd always thought that they defined a safe place, when what they really defined was a limit.

Rosemary spit an arc of water onto her stomach, then tried harder to hit a more worthy spot. She whipped open her legs wider than was efficient. She rolled onto her back. The cool air pricked her nipples. Bubbles burst between her legs.

She tucked and stood waist deep in the pool. She paced, working hard, as if she were trying to regain the use of her limbs after injury. Birth, the coming of age, marriage, death—all were noted with ceremony. Where, she wondered, was the ritual for dissolution? There is no service. No one sends flowers, or even a card. Other women clutch their husbands and eventually just stop calling.

Her thighs tired. Sometimes the water felt heavy, felt like cement. She felt like cement. She skimmed her forearms along its surface. Like that, her hands came up to cup heavy breasts, and her thoughts traveled not just to Phil, but to Babette and Stevie B. This body she gave to them, and without hesitation. This body—theirs to transform. Her hands continued down past jellied abdomen and she plied her fingers, grateful for lubrication. After a time, she slipped under and lay against the

pool's rough bottom, where she thrust and thrust her
fingers to the beat of her heart.

When she surfaced, coughing, choking, and only mar-
ginally sated, she found the moon her partner, and Buck
her witness, standing under the arch of the solarium.

The door banged. Rosemary set the bags down heavily on the counter. I'm home, she wanted them to know.
Finish whatever you're doing. At least, be discreet.
Show some respect. In the short hot steps from the station wagon to the house, the straps of her handbag had
cut deep grooves. Her blouse stuck to her back.

She glanced across the patio to Babette's window.
Were they here? Was he? Had he really seen her last
night? Had he seen everything? Babette's door to the
deck was shut. No darting shadows, no muted giggling.
Perhaps they weren't home. Perhaps they had gone to
the lake. That's where she would be on a day like this,
if she were a teenager. She stepped out of her wedgies.
The cool linoleum soothed. But where was Stevie B? No
need to panic. Stevie. OK, yes. Steven was at a friend's.
She had dropped him off after picking him up at Phil's.
Was that just this morning?

She poured herself a drink and then another as she
unloaded the perishables into the refrigerator, making
space for two half-gallons of real ice cream. Without
thinking, without breaking stride, she reached for the

phone and made call after call. Her invitation was finally accepted by new neighbors already around the corner since winter without Rosemary having offered much more than a smile and a good-morning wave. Kiki Martin. Jeffrey Martin. Two girls under six with glasses. A golden retriever. "Bring your suits," she'd said. "We'll barbecue."

The front door opened and closed. Babette called out lifelessly, "Hi, Mom."

Rosemary wasn't fooled. Babette hadn't just arrived; more likely Buck had probably just left. Maybe he was avoiding her, too. Good.

Rosemary kissed her daughter without inhaling too deeply. If the girl still smelled of their encounter, she didn't want to know. Not today.

"Thought you shopped on Tuesday."

"Ran out of milk. And we're having company."

Babette groaned to hear who company was.

"You can eat and run."

"Buck invited?"

"Always." Rosemary hoped her voice was even. She stopped herself from adding that they were having steak. Buck loved steak.

She stripped the silk off a dozen ears of corn, wrapped each in foil, scrubbed half a bag of potatoes and set them to boil. Asked her daughter what she did that day. Babette offered some vague summer answer commensurate with her mother's true interest.

The girl peeled off to go to her room. Moments later, music from The Doors blasted from her record player. *You know that it would be untrue / You know that I would be a liar / If I was to say to you / Girl, we couldn't get much higher.* Rosemary imagined Babette on her bed, but naked, on top of her bedspread, and was grateful the girl's bedroom did not face the street. She felt fatigued from the gathering still to come and longed to lie down in a dark, cool place.

Things that have been around for a while have a way of disappearing, like people. After a while, a person can just stop seeing that once favorite vase, the jewelry box carried back from the perfect honeymoon. She was often startled when someone new would come over and comment. Kiki Martin was the kind of woman to comment on everything, and touch as much as she could get away with. *What a darling Florentine box,* Rosemary could already hear her chirp. *Jeffrey got me one of those on our honeymoon, too.* And Rosemary would see the box for the first time in years and be compelled to answer, *Yes, it is nice, isn't it?* even though she and Phil hadn't been able to afford Europe until their tenth anniversary, when suddenly they could afford it every year. When they become better acquainted, Kiki Martin would be the kind of woman to open drawers and cabinets, saying, *I've always wanted to see inside one of these, you don't mind, do you?* And Rosemary would let her, too astounded to be able to recall those simple declarative words, *Yes, I do mind.*

Stop, as she would find herself once again paralyzed into silence.

How different things might be, how very different, if she had been able to say to Phil even once, *Phil, please. Don't do this.*

Rosemary pulled out her blouse and stepped out of her skirt. She needed to lie down, just for a bit, take some time, have a bath. She drew the curtains and dropped her watch and charm bracelet on the nightstand.

Across the patio came the basso lure of Jim Morrison. *Before you slip into unconsciousness / I'd like to have another kiss.* From where she lay on the bed, she could see straight through the doorway to her dressing room: the head block askew; the fall askew and unkempt, as if hurriedly replaced; her poplin skirt and madras shirt jammed in between the winter navies, clothes Babette shunned as being sexless; saw her strand of pearls preventing the Florentine box from closing. And in the middle distance she could make out in the carpet four crisp, square indentations left by the legs of Grandma Berg's floral armchair, which now sat alongside. She thought she could still smell them after they had done whatever they had been doing, in the chair, the girl in *her* skirt, *her* madras shirt, *her* cascading fall—when Rosemary interrupted them with her untimely return.

The music stopped, revealing the latent thumping she had mistaken for an approaching headache. Rosemary willed her attention to her Florentine box, focusing on the ocher and olive and gold leaf defining the box's complex curves, seeking in color and line and texture some sorry refuge from the heat in the house.

The sultry evening had been made all the stickier by Rosemary's ironing. Buck hadn't been around for a couple of days and, yes, she missed him but not the ease his absence gave her. He's separating from them, from all of them, readying himself for college, the world. She wanted that to be the reason. She wanted to doubt that she had indeed seen him that night, to doubt that he had really seen her.

Babette sighed. She sat in the breakfast nook, her feet on the vinyl, toes spread with cotton puffs. She wiggled them.

"Mom, why don't you go out with Heidi's dad? He's only asked you like three times." She added under her breath, "I bet he's good size."

Rosemary spritzed both sides of the sheet. "Don't talk about men like that, honey."

"Why not? They talk about us like that." Babette blew on her toenails. "We wonder what kissing them would be like, we wonder whether they'll have hair on their behinds—why can't we talk about it?"

"There are many things we do in private, things we may say or think, all private. I don't have to spell them out for you. People don't talk about these things."

"What if I have questions? Who'm I going to ask?"

"What questions? Which?"

"How can you stand it, Mom? You haven't had a man in over two years. Why don't you move on, get yourself another guy?"

Is that how she thinks of her father, just another guy to discard and replace? Her own father? Is that what she'll do, the minute she gets bored?

Babette chewed on her knee. "I hear you, Mom. At night."

Some nights it was a book being closed too emphatically, or the chink of one ice cube against another. It was no longer crying.

On one of those perfect summer evenings when the night inspired lazy strolls, the slow eating of ice cream, lying barefoot on the porch swing while saying not much—the kind of night when being with the other was its own reward—it was on this kind of night that Rosemary set fire to Phil's things. The family room door slammed open. From the weight of the footfalls, she knew that the first one out was Buck. She wished she had thought to wait until Thursday, when she was alone. She should have waited, should have tried. Some things are like that, consuming, like a fire: a match, a flare, a great deal of fuel, and you want to stop it but you don't know how. She stood upwind with a firm grip on a can of lighter fluid, her face reflecting the flames' dervish red. Letters from judges and senators, a diving medal strung through with grosgrain, an oak swivel chair stolen from the law library that Phil had for over twenty years. Near the steps were slightly singed framed photos, a last-minute change of heart. One showed the Bergs, cradling their babies, fearless with youth. Babette lay a hand on her brother's shoulder. Buck ran over and kicked away several cans of shaving foam before they could explode. He was curbside when the firemen arrived and he talked with them sparingly. As if to make the firemen go, he pulled out the garden hose and doused the remaining embers. The firemen showed admirable restraint. Babette turned Stevie B back toward the house.

Rosemary flipped and rotated the sheet and started pressing the other side. The fabric sizzled. "I think you should mind your own business, young lady."

"Is this going to happen to me when I get old? Are they going to leave me, too?"

Rosemary stopped ironing. Her child was sitting, arms wrapped around knees. Rosemary knew what she should do. She should go around the ironing board. Envelop her daughter. Kiss her tight.

"I look like you, don't I? Like when you were young, like when you and Daddy first met. I catch him looking at me sometimes."

There was a time when both mother and daughter delighted in wearing the same outfits, the same winter coats, stitched by Rosemary with matching anchor buttons and satin linings. She would gaze down, smitten, and Babette would glance up, her perfect little hand feeling so right in Rosemary's own. In time, Babette blossomed and developed a style Rosemary likened to a breath of fresh air, an inspiration, a signature so individual that in later years, Rosemary found a return to imitation nothing short of appropriation. And finally, an affront.

"If you took better care of yourself—look at you, Mom, I mean, look even at your hair. Daddy's right, you just don't pay attention anymore."

Rosemary lifted the sheet high to keep it from dragging on the floor. "Something wrong with the way I look?"

"You look fine. Just, you don't look, I don't know. Like you used to."

"I bathe every day. I tweeze unwanted hairs. My clothes are clean and pressed." No matter how thick her waist had become with children, Rosemary had always displayed it proudly, her woman's body, her honor.

Babette eyed the skirt and blouse. "You used to stand out."

Rosemary managed to stop herself from saying, *Like you?*

"Outfits from Magnin's, a weekly trip to the hairdresser—that would have kept your father from leaving you and Steven and me?"

Babette spoke into her knee. "Daddy didn't leave me. Not me. Not Stevie."

"Opening night, *Million Dollar Mermaids,* where was he?"

Babette pulled the puffs from between her toes and wadded them into a ball.

"Your first-time solo. That dive off the high board into that hoop of fire. Took my breath away."

"Daddy was taking a deposition—"

"—You don't believe that? You, of all people. You're so sophisticated." Rosemary pointed with the tip of the iron. "Your father was a no-show. The worst kind of loser."

She had promised herself she would not malign the father to the children. She had promised herself. Rosemary put the iron down but she did not let go.

"You're married for twenty years to a man you loved enough to make a family together, and this perfect man leaves you—could you just move on to the next available guy? Could you?"

"How'm I supposed to know, Mom? I haven't even lived twenty years."

"That's right. You don't know. You can't know. Twenty years—that's half a lifetime."

The sheets were coming out good tonight, the corners were not at all askew.

"Whatever your father wanted. Law school, real property, a new Jaguar every year, me. He wanted me. Phil Berg, Olympic alternate, my own Johnny Weissmuller. You know he stole me away from another man? Don't turn away, miss. You're the one who wanted to talk about every private thing."

"Amanda says—"

"—In my bed, Amanda, where I nursed you, where Steven was conceived—"

The girl shook her head.

"No? How about my sheets stinking of Chantilly? I don't wear Chantilly. Do you?"

Babette's breath caught.

"Not even that big," Rosemary whispered, squeezing a thumb and forefinger together until they almost touched. "Amanda. Smaller than an aspirin, less shiny than the glint in her father's eyes, when Phil and I got married. Amanda. Still cooks you spaghetti sauce from a jar? Lets you try her lipstick? Tucks Steven in? God! To think of her hands all over him."

The iron was so hot Babette could smell it.

"Daddy's gonna marry her."

Rosemary whacked the fruit bowl right off the table.

Babette glanced at the broken crockery and slid off the table, mindful of her bare feet. She managed to salvage a cantaloupe and a couple of apples, and swept the rest into the garbage. Rosemary tried to reach out. The girl was careful not to bump her as she passed.

"Show me how you like it."

In twenty years of making love to Phil and only to

Phil, never once had he asked her how she liked it. He had little genuine interest after he came, but Buck was patient. Patient or proud. He was eager to start again after he rested.

She could have stopped. He came in. He shut the door. She said—what did she say? "No, not you." And he said? He said, "Why not me? I'm as good as the next guy." "I had Phil. I don't want just any next guy." "No, you don't. You want me. You've been watching me, waiting for me." She tried to laugh him off. "You're practically family, one of the neighborhood children." Children! She didn't mean to say that, calling him a child. Could she take it back?

"Look at me, Rosemary."

He called her Rosemary! As if he were a man. In her ear, he said it, entering her so easily, like this, whispering.

Had she thought to say, *No, not here. Not in this house. Not in this bed.* How could she say it happened too fast? Six paces from the door to the bed—a near eternity. Buck covered her and she could feel only how right it was, and the horror of them lying down together was infinitely containable, as containable as him lying here in this same bed with Babette, as containable as Phil on his knees, and the generous offering of Amanda's back-side—*anything you want, Phil.* She could have stopped—*whatever Rosie won't do.* She had all those half-seconds, those lovely, ratcheted moments as Buck lifted her hem and lowered his lips to kiss her there and there and there until she was thinking *hurry* so hard she couldn't tell which woman's voice it was she heard cry out.

Did she love him? His was the face she had seen in her windshield, on her ceiling late at night, when Heidi's father so boldly took her knee at dinner. Two more weeks and Buck would have been gone. She could have made it. After that moonlit swim, she had tried to stay away from the house whenever he was over. Other days, she hadn't been so generous.

She hadn't planned for this to happen, hadn't meant for it to be Buck. She flexed her toes back toward her heart until her calves burned. Perhaps Phil hadn't planned to fall in love with Amanda. Who, after all, sits down to plan such destruction?

Rosemary took a drag on her cigarette, holding in her scorching breath as if it could keep her from drowning. Midnight. The deck lights shut off. The pool floated in the dark, lit by underwater beams.

Rosemary closed the doors to the patio. She longed to lie down, if sleep would only come. He would tell Babette. Dear god, would he? Would Buck tell Babette? Rosemary picked her blouse off the floor. If Babette had to find out, better it be from her. After all, she was the one adult. She fluffed the sheets, she mitered corners. Yes, and what would she say? Just what part of this night did she understand well enough to talk about it?

The door opened. Buck walked in, startling them both.

Hadn't he left?

Wasn't she sleeping?

Rosemary couldn't move, even to close her robe. He bent to search for socks and shoes. She wanted to say something. Speak, Rosemary, speak. Two lives depend on it. Say his name, anything. Buck looked up, and just as quickly looked away again. Speak? What could they say? They couldn't even look at each other.

Like that, he was gone.

On his way out he locked the front door. The room chilled before it occurred to her to run after him, to see what she could do to help him.

One day he will confess this night to a special woman. Rosemary could imagine him, a man of forty, a father himself, sitting in an unlit car with the one he loved, a woman not the mother of his children. It would be after a particularly intimate evening, one to make a person think an accumulation of such encounters was not only possible, but inevitable, and right. He would hold his car keys in his hand before starting the engine and his woman would be attentive, ready to receive his soul. He would tell her then, head down, voice low, so she would not mistake the depths of his failings: I went to see my girlfriend and when she wasn't home, I fucked the mother. He would tell it just like that, sparing no one. Daring her to love him still. Needing it.

In one motion, Rosemary stripped the linens from the bed and stuffed the whole mess into the hamper. When she straightened up, she was startled to see this perfect stranger in the vanity. She stepped up close and examined every vein, every sag and fold, and saw herself anew through Buck's green eyes.

Divining the Waters

Aquamarine, and one cannot see where the waters end or where they begin. Four, ten, twenty strokes underwater, and when I surface I am alone with the night. Where the shore had been now there is only water. Water, as far as I can see. Water, all around. Where is north? Which way to land? The water swells, it swirls. I'm swirling. It twists and shouts, it lifts me on broad shoulders, it stands up on hind legs, only to collapse under its own cumulative weight, but not before dragging me under.

The cold wakes me, the heat, my own heat, my labored breathing. Stan also has a deviated septum, but he's deaf to his own percussion. Can separate beds be far off? Open water, my personal bête. The clock hand sweeps: 1 A.M. I have slept two hours and fifteen minutes. Ted upstairs has a new lover. Her name is Nancy Nancy Nancy. In a flash, I see that Rosemary Berg was also sleepless those first months after Phil left her, and certainly after that night in August 1971, when she succumbed to a moment of overwhelming weakness and entered into a mutual seduction with the boyfriend of her teenage daughter. His name was Billy Buckman, and we all called him Buck.

Burt Lancaster is swimming home. He wears a gold band ring and sleek black trunks. Go, Burt. I shut the door to the bedroom so the TV won't wake Stan. Yesterday's coffee warms my hands. My robe falls open. Burt looks good. He was fifty-four in '67 and more than holding his own. The movie plays on late-night cable, is called *The Swimmer,* and was recast from the metal of a Cheever story. I could work, cast some silver of my own, but I'd rather watch Burt dive. Burt's Neddy Merrill journeys barefoot from one backyard to another, swims some laps, then continues on to the next pool and the next rendezvous with the past in his aquaquest for home, and it is clear to everyone but him that when he finally arrives, his Ithaka will be a shambles and his Penelope long gone.

The Plunge is what we call the pool closest to us. I can walk to it and do, even in the dead of winter when daybreak is an hour away. Seven days a week, every week of the year: my day begins with water. Traveling east a half-mile, there's the fountain at Arlington Circle. A frog could swim in it but not me, though it is plenty large for an entire family to drown. Continuing up the

hill toward the ridge, there's a pool on Fairlawn surrounded by rolling greens and climbing roses, ideal for
afternoon weddings and children's circuses. But Berkeley isn't warm enough for private pools to be common.
Unlike Burt's Neddy Merrill, who circumswam his fic-
tional county in a day, I would have to hike up a ridge
and cross a canyon to link my city pool to the one in
Rosemary's Orinda backyard.

"You can't swim there," Stan says. "And even if you
could, there'd be no U-shaped house, no cabana, no
pool access from every room—contractors just do not
put exterior doors in children's bedrooms."

Stan knows I don't really mean to swim to Rosemary's. But their house could be like I imagined, with
the hearth at the center of the U and all the rooms facing each other. It could be like that. It's not that Stan
lacks a certain imagination, but he's an exacting man.
Permanence, dovetail joints, copper piping—these are
his standards.

Her pool cleaner snaked across the surface, sucking
up leaves and the colossal blossom. As Babette and Stevie B sat down at Phil and Amanda's table, Rosemary
got up from the lawn chaise where she had been watching the changing light, and she prepared something un-
spectacular: a chop, an ear of corn, dinner for one. The
front door opened. She looked up, holding a brick of
peas. Buck stood in her door. She continued to cook,
only more of it. He set the table with the hot dishes she

prepared. They sat in the breakfast nook opposite each other. After a few bites, she pushed her plate away and lit a cigarette. When she reached for her gin, he dissuaded her. A glance was all it took. Two days' growth on his face, shirt partially unbuttoned, and as he set his fork down, a slight trembling that betrayed his veneer of cool. When she got up, he followed half a step behind. He put an arm around her waist and a wave rolled over her body that made her sick and breathless at the same time and she nearly said, *Stop.* After the deed was done, while her bed was still warm with him and with her, wet with him and with her, he picked up the extension in her unlit kitchen and called his friend Denny. *I just made the mother.*

"He didn't say that. Not while he was in her house. Not right afterward."

"Yeah. He did."

Stan stares at me. He walks out of the room.

You tell someone a bad enough dream, sooner or later it becomes their nightmare, too. This explains a lot of denial. Maybe Stan'd like to know that Buck struggled for weeks before giving in; or that it was an instinctive act—Babette wasn't home but, hey, Rosemary was. Or, perhaps he saw what they could do together as a gift from him to her, offered with that same awkward bravado that Phil might hand a beggar a five-dollar bill. Or this: that Buck hadn't considered the consequences—

who does at eighteen? And as Rosemary Berg could tell you, to ponder the consequences, one has the rest of one's life.

The sentence starts out innocently enough. "I just made the—" We are fine up to here. I could put a hundred different endings on this sentence and have it come out decent: "I just made the *drinks*" (which Buck refused to do even when the Bergs were still a family); or, "I just made the *team*" (effortlessly achieved in his sophomore year); or, "I just made the *best decision of my life*" (something Rosemary had hoped to hear each of her charges say at least once in their lives). But, "I just made the *mother*"—appropriating the very noun that conjures up a safe house of a woman, nuclear family, wag-tail dog, fried chicken, summers in Carmel, and cocoa by the fire—this is a line from a horror movie.

Change even one of those other words and the sentence would be easier to take. For instance, the confessional *I*. But, where does the bowed head of confession begin, and the neon tail of bravado end? How less harsh might it have been if, say, Buck's friend had told the story, because his friend did tell the story, about five heartbeats after hearing it from Buck on the phone, as if he had just killed someone, and could Denny please come over and wipe the knife for prints. But Denny didn't say, "Buck just made the mother." He said, "That was Buck." Then he finished the roach before continuing:

"Buck said, 'I just made the mother.'" Then Denny rolled away from me as if *I* had been the one who had done the unconscionable.

Or consider, please, the wet-paint immediacy of the *just,* like Buck couldn't leave Rosemary's bed fast enough to broadcast the news and his, what?—pride? fear? shame?—he felt, and with whom?—himself? her? the both of them? or with whatever pain drove them together in the first place?

Now, *made*—that love generation term went far to deromanticize the union of two people ecstatic enough about each other to join their bodies in such protean fluids, bra burning, *hell no we won't go,* and late-twentieth-century hallucinogenic, fleet, hungry, anonymous sex. (Do I remember all their names? Do I?) *Made*—as if until Buck came along Rosemary Berg had been unwhole, this woman who had brought to her marriage her modest family money and her abundant managerial skills, both of which put Phil comfortably through law school; this woman who had carried each of his children inside her for the better part of the year; this woman who had sworn in a consecrated place in front of fifty witnesses, *till death*. I know I stayed with Stan because in twenty years he has never used the word *made* followed by a personal pronoun when referring to what we did together, or even thought of as something *he did to me,* in the bed, out of the bed, driving down the highway, or alongside spreads of cactus when we were once so urgent.

Now, every word in this razor-studded cudgel has been covered except for the most chilling: the definite article *the*. Not "I just made *her* mother," but "I just made *the* mother." With this one little word, the woman who had welcomed Buck into her family and fed him and chauffeured him and cheered him on to first- and second-place wins and encouraged labored essays and instinctively knew when to let him be, this woman who had just taken his body into her own and so openly, with such overwhelming desire and joy that she cried real tears—with this one word, Rosemary Berg had been objectified and reduced to the generic: *the mother.* Yet, it specified Mrs. Berg as the only mother in question. A triumph in false anonymity.

Denny walked out of the bedroom and I realized that there was a starkness to American explicitness with language that I, as an immigrant, hadn't begun to understand. English didn't seem such a great improvement over the implicit, convoluted obscurity of my own Cantonese. But, please, let me not blame the language for how my people use it.

"How would the Chinese say it? How would you, Stan?"

"Me? *Me?* I wouldn't say anything. Nothing. Because I would never do such a thing."

Never do such a thing.

How instinctively we dive into the twin pillboxes of the absolute, and the vague. *Never. Such a thing.*

In 1972, the summer of my sophomore year—a year after the grand seduction—I was the claims girl in an office in Chinatown. Auto, reports in triplicate, a quick dispatch to an adjuster. Cases involving B.I. required a medical report. The older Chinese distrusted the phone. They came to the office and took a seat. They carried their policies, they crossed their ankles. "Man ran into me! *He* ran into *me!* 'Chinks! Why you don't learn to drive!'" Halfway through their report, Buck slipped into the office and hovered over my shoulder, speaking low, so low, a murmur—*I just made*—"Stoplight, I stop, what I do wrong? Not my fault"—*just made the*—"Why he talk like that?"—*mother the mother*—

"—Pardon me? Pardon?" I had to ask the Fongs to repeat themselves, inadvertently giving them more reason to think that being rear-ended was truly incomprehensible.

Buck's no bigger than a G.I. Joe. Sometimes he's just the noise in the air intake. Through the years he arrives unannounced—at my table, in the workshop, late at night—and always he says the same one thing. With that one line, Buck laid out Rosemary Berg for all of us to see. With that one line, and the ones that follow: *Teats to here. Varicose veins. The woman really let herself go.* I can't help but wonder how past lovers might splay me out in other people's imaginations, and if I were now to come face-to-face with these other versions of myself, could I find anything that I could claim had once been mine, and lost?

"That wasn't his real name. Buck? Really?"

"And he wasn't the only Buck I knew. The other one was an upright butcher, worked for Lenny, hunted in season and dressed his own. Yes, that was his real name."

What's in a name? Everything. I am Ruby. My older sisters were Jade and Emerald. More precious, more rare, more desirable to the gods, they became part of the national statistic for neonatal mortality. My parents learned well. *Don't shout,* they said, *don't call attention. Work hard, wash daily, steal no shoes, stay out of jail. If the gods don't claim you, the foreign demon Americans will. Dirty Chinks.* Semiprecious Ruby, not even Pearl.

Stan isn't Stan's real name, it's the name on his naturalization papers. His mother named him after the explorer, that's the kind of future she saw for him. Not to get mixed up with a stay-at-home like me. She never imagined Stan as daring but he is, in his own way. When I say *Stan,* I want you to think of all the great Stans and Stanleys in the world. I want you to think of a lyric tenor sax man; or a formidable left-handed slugger of another era; or the man who patented a quick way of clearing the table and could call out for a woman in such a way as to alert a whole city block to his feeling for her; or the young explorer who, after Dr. Livingstone, went into deep Africa and found the source of the Nile. How many people can tally up their lives and say they had once gone into uncharted territories looking for where life begins? Stan the Man. All Stans. I stayed with Stan these many years even though he didn't play the saxophone, and would never be Herb Wong and comment in a browning voice on the onetime world-class, mother of all jazz stations. I stayed with him because even though we've rarely ventured beyond the Rockies, he's never failed to impress me with his unerring sense of north. I stayed with him even though he would never lose himself and call out for me with such possession that neighbors would be both repelled and envious. Unlike Phil Berg, Stan's not going to run off to find himself at forty-three. My Stan has always known who he was and just how he felt about things. And I am imprisoned in the safety of his love.

Stevie B said he was sitting across the street (because he was allowed to go around the corner but not to cross the street), and for the better part of an hour he watched Buck carry boxes from the curb into his new house, before dragging him home to see his Lab puppy with the enormous feet. "No, no, no," Phil insisted. "*I* found Buck outside the hardware store after he put his fist through the window; isn't he our neighbor, and aren't we, as parents, supposed to look out for *all* the children?" Babette licked the chocolate icing off her finger and said, "He asked me where I lived but I didn't tell him, Mom."

Rosemary counted out fourteen candles and said that Buck came to her door a wet eleven and glanced past her to the placid pool on the other side of the atrium; that Babette hid in her room and changed her suit several times before coming out in a white piqué bikini trimmed in red rickrack, and she was nine; that Stevie B was five and raced Buck to the deck, where they did cannonballs solid for an hour; that Buck ate every snack she set out on the patio table and returned the next afternoon to see if he could sustain the dream. And because her story was infused with more detail, the family secretly conceded to her version.

Buck would say that he was swimming his way through the neighborhood as the pool at his new house was unfinished. By traveling in an ever-widening circle and targeting a different house each day, he thought to avoid wearing out his welcome and stay out of trouble until the end of summer. Never did he expect to meet a Rosemary Berg, or to have his childhood handed back to him. But, no one asked Buck for his version. Instead they sang. They said, *Make a wish and blow.* Then they put their hands together and clapped.

He came every day that summer and his place at Rosemary's table was everyone's assumption. He didn't have to be funny or smart; he just had to behave, knowing that without blood security, they could, at any time, just shut the door. But he saw the way they all looked at him, and told himself things would be all right if he just didn't mess up. His was a beauty as exotic and arresting as he himself was shy.

"How can Buck be shy? How can he do what he did and say what he said and you try to tell me he was shy?"

"Well, he was, Stan. He would hardly look you in the eye. Then when he did—and it would be for only a second—it just about knocked you over."

The toast crunches in his mouth. "You mean, it just about knocked *you* over."

"Yeah, I guess it did, and guess what, it had that effect on everyone, men, women, children, dogs—no one was immune."

"He must have been some looker."

Stan is showering and I have to suppress my shock. Does body hair go gray? I check myself. A *white* hair, stiff as wire—did that come out of me? I yank. It hurts.

"He was messed up, Stan, what do you want me to say? He was a runaway, to a home with a mom and a dad and chores and siblings, but still a runaway. He stole, he cut class, used foul language, kissed the girls and broke their green, green hearts."

Bags under my eyes again, dark and pouchy. Even acupuncture has no lasting effect. Falling asleep isn't the problem, it's staying asleep. Dr. Ou says a complete REM cycle is about three hours, that a person needs only nine or ten a week to function properly. One could have five straight nights of hell and two six-hour teases and still function, according to Dr. Ou. I'm functioning—but is that living?

"Actually, the only thing Buck did with any seriousness was smoke dope and dive. And this kid could hardly talk."

"He's no kid, he's the same age as you."

"I haven't seen him in twenty-some years. In my mind he's still a teenager."

Stan's in a lather, holding a razor. "So. When are you going to get back to work instead of obsessing about this *kid?*"

When we first notice them—boys, men—we love them straight off for their otherness, their hardness where we are soft, their bulk and breadth and the way they smell, the way their bodies claim space. We marvel that their minds can travel down the same paths as ours, yet somehow manage to reach destinations we hadn't begun to imagine. They fill us with nothing short of wonder. If they look at us longer than ten seconds, it's all over. That look works its way down into our DNA and we know we'd forfeit our ancestral lands for their undying attention. The years pass, and this same otherness that once drew us to them suddenly seems abrasive, and we wonder why on earth can't they be more like us, need like us, respond like us. Talk like us. Then one fall day, when even our bones have begun to crack, we wake up and wonder just who it is we have taken into our arms, invited into our most intimate chambers.

"Marry me," Stan whispers in a moment of heat. Meaning he wants me to have his baby. I don't want to have his baby. I don't want to have anyone's baby. He's been saying this for so many years, he's lost sight of the fact that time has just about run out for me. Or maybe he's only too aware.

"I like it how it is, Stan. If I marry you, we'll have a houseful of kids because we'll think we're so lucky we can or that the next one will be perfect because the first one was, or wasn't, and then I'll wake up one morning ballasted with three under ten, and you'll have run off with some woman whose two-car garage you just converted to a honeymoon suite."

"Well, I can run off with her now."

"Sure you can."

"Well?"

"So, go. If that's what you have to do."

We're nose-to-nose.

"I think you're afraid."

I back up.

"You're afraid you're going to fail your children."

Stan's right. I am afraid. I've always been afraid that I might turn out like one of them, but not just Rosemary. Phil. I'm afraid I could be like Phil. Or Babette—three children with three different men. Or Stevie B, laughing one minute, a human projectile the next, and when he landed in the intersection, two cars missed him but not the third. His voice was changing, he was becoming a man. You could have heard it in his moan.

Stan puts those hammer hands on my shoulders, thinking his weight alone will hold me to earth. "It's not going to happen."

"How do you know? How can you possibly know?"

He drops his hands. I'm frustrating him, it's all so easy now. It doesn't even occur to me to wonder how to avoid it.

"You're right. I don't know any more than you can know that you'll fail. We all make mistakes, but we'll get through it."

"Some mistakes are OK? Where's this list?"

"There is no list."

"A child falling off the roof?"

"Boys climb roofs. Some of them fall."

"What if he breaks his neck?"

Stan throws the magazine across the room. "We're not these people. We don't even know them! She messed up!"

"Yes. She did."

"And you don't think that's wrong?"

"Of course I do. I think she did, too. And still, it happened. Now, I need to understand that, how even someone like Rosemary Berg could make that kind of mistake."

"Let it go. You'll never know."

He's right. I'll never know. But that doesn't mean I can forget about it.

I haven't had a decent new idea in weeks. Stan says just make the timeless top ten that always sell, simple rings with simple stones. I'm not a machine. What's the point in handmade if there are five hundred of them? What exactly would be the point?

"The point is to pay for the electricity that drives the motor on the buffer that shines your silver. Christmas is just a few months away. Stop thinking about that woman."

The man leads with his head, a slow, forward urging. He wears the mismatched discards from the FREE box, using for a cape a sleeping bag of royal blue. From the moment he wakes until he passes out in his cardboard shelter, the prince of the flowing robe walks. People part to give him room, they avert their eyes. He walks and mutters words that are recognizably English, but whose syntax is all his own.

Stan's older sister, Amy, never learned to drive. Everywhere she goes, she walks: to work, to shop (which she does daily, as if she were still living in Hong Kong), to meet her married lover, to the campus for cultural events, to Chinatown for tea. Through the years we have offered to teach her to drive, but she insists on her contentment. Last week I saw her marching down Shattuck

Avenue but I didn't tell Stan, because then I would have had to tell him that I hesitated because Amy was talking to herself, and with great feeling.

Marley, who guards at the Plunge, says the shoes need to be rotated. She herself has three pairs of endorsed sneakers. A backpack keeps her hands free; a can of mace is primed in her holster. As she walks, she replays every confrontation she has had in the last fifteen years and reworks the dialogue so that in the end it comes out good.

There's the old man with dark glasses and a dirty bandage where his nose used to be. He's not Chinese but he's some kind of rice eater. On a flush day he hawks day-old news. I give him a dollar for something that was delivered yesterday for thirty-seven cents, and I wonder where's his family, where's his nose, what's wrong with his eyes, and what would Stan say if I were to bring him home for dinner?

These walkers shuffle past my stand, past the bank, the Laundromat, a few even have rooms on lower University, where with the aid of one substance or another they can ignore around them the commerce of sex. All day long they wander the streets, they natter and declaim. They wake me in the dead of night and I confuse them with the rebels in the book-burning world of Bradbury—those tomes on legs. But the walkers in my town recite daily, from endpaper to endpaper, from once upon a time until the last good-bye, defending against oblivion not the great books of literature, but the ballad of their own life story.

In Bradbury's world of book burning, of the suppression of all story—story as art, as history, as witness, as inquiry, as explication, as science, as luminous guides of faith—the times are so incendiary that Bradbury takes for a title the temperature at which books ignite. If 451 degrees Fahrenheit is the temperature at which corporeal stories burn, at what temperature, Stan, does the soul burn? What temperature, memory?

A man pushes his face into mine. His fingers are filthy, a complex brown crusted with everything he has come into contact with. "How much is that there nose ring?"

He coughs and I try not to think TB.

"It's yours." It wasn't a nose ring, but I wasn't going to tell him where he could or couldn't hang it.

He waits for me to wrap it as he has watched me wrap other purchases. When I hand him his ring, I can't help but touch his fingers, and I try hard not to flinch and try harder to look him in the eye. His head bobs continuously, as if he were no longer the master of himself. He whirls back around and pokes the air between us. "I'm *watching* you, lady."

That night I am awakened by the insistent call of my own heartbeat.

"I think I saw Rosemary today."

"Rosemary who?"

"Berg. Rosemary Berg. What other Rosemary do I know?"

"You don't even know that one; how could you recognize her?"

"She was walking between Moe's and the metaphysical bookstore."

"A bookstore can't be metaphysical."

"You know what I mean. It was her."

"And how old was this woman?"

"Sixty-something, seventy. Still beautiful." Beautiful. Haunted. All these years of sitting out on the avenue, my skin has leathered, my hands are a wreck—chapped, skinned, scorched, and just plain dirty—but Rosemary Berg still looks good.

"You never said she was beautiful. You said t—"

"—I know what I said. I said what someone said to his friend, who then said to me. She was beautiful."

"How do you know?"

"I know. Phil Berg would not marry a woman who was not beautiful."

Stan pulls out a pocket reference that I've never seen him use, one that lists the melting points of nine thousand compounds and the optimum time of year to plant beans. "Says here that the woman you saw had as much chance of being Rosemary Berg as the sun does of burning out in our great-grandchildren's lifetime."

"It was her. I know it."

"I think you should stick to your baubles."

Baubles. Stan thinks I've been on the avenue too long, the scene has hardened ("Fred Cody has died, so has Moe; one of these days someone will stick a knife under your chin"); that I should have gone back to school long ago, or gone to Germany, or North Africa, or Taxco, or wherever one goes to study with masters of silversmithing. He thinks I should have moved my stuff inside. Inside pieces have more concept, more execution, more precious stones; but with a bigger price tag comes a much smaller market. Some people want that exclusivity, but I think everyone needs a little bit of beauty, don't you?

Too many hours spent working alone and I need to hear live voices. I need to be here, on the street, in the same way I need to be in water, in the same way other people need to walk and walk and walk. I need to be around other makers and vendors—who have become some kind of family. Suki—owner of a baseball bat and a Hasselblad by which she makes her living—is my librarian. She loans me books, Italians named di Lampedusa, Levi, Calvino ("You still reading *Invisible Cities*?" "Not still. *Again*. I'm reading it *again*.")

Here on the street, I can look into the eyes of the people who buy my pieces, I can see the texture of their skin. They try on everything, they tell their stories, and expect from me nothing more than my rapt attention: "Momma died last month, what a relief"; "I haven't had sex with my husband in nine years but he's a good man"; "Me and Jesus talked last night. He loves me. Oh yeah."

Phil hocked his trumpet to buy Rosemary a wedding ring. Even his jilted roommate had thought that that was a goddamned romantic thing to do.

Burt Lancaster's Neddy Merrill continued to wear his wedding band long after his spouse had left him, as did Rosemary Berg—two solid cases of denial.

The dowry of Muslim silver rarely lasted more than a generation, as upon death, a woman's collection is melted down and remade into jewels for a new bride. Perhaps taking a cue from the Muslims, Phil had his wedding band recast into something more to Amanda's liking, as if recasting the metal could obliterate the story and each long year of loving.

The Chinese prefer gold: 22 karat, ultra yellow, soft as butter gold. My mother gave me three flawless jades set in 22 karat, for me and for my daughters (or wives of sons). They sit in a box in my drawer, durable testaments to my every failing.

The walls of the city pools are painted with murals. The one at the Plunge is animated with mermen and sirens, green-and-blue fish-people, who at night slide off the buildings into the pool and swim out to sea, artful and effortless, whereas before they had been merely upright. I am shoeless in a gauzy silk dress the likes of which I have never owned. Not a sound, not even a breeze. Stan scoops me in his arms and swirls me in water up to his chest. Oh yes, we laugh. Sometimes it's a lake, sometimes it's the ocean. The dress is somewhat the same, the action always the same. Stan slips under, lifts me up, and carries me off bareback as I cling to his dorsal fin. The green sea tints the hem of my dress, seeps up the folds, makes for my heart, and I am mesmerized by the beauty of capillary actions.

Babette swam her daily miles in laps and flip-turns and racing dives. At 5:30 in the morning Rosemary would sit in her icebox of a station wagon, cocooned in Sears' best plaid sleeping bag, her hands wrapped around successive cups of steaming coffee as she waited out Babette's practice. Rosemary could have gone back home and returned like other moms, but she thought if Babette had to get up while her tender body cried for sleep, if she had to work out for an hour and a half before school, pushing herself so hard she sometimes threw up her cornflakes, then the least Rosemary could do was tough it out with her.

And yet, Rosemary had also been this other kind of woman: one who could fall in love with one man while in the arms of another. Roommates and best friends, the men were also teammates and rivals in competition, swimming for Cal Berkeley. Phil came home late one night forgetting he had told his roommate that he wouldn't be home all weekend. Rosemary was jack-knifed between the wall and her fiancé, with both legs off the floor. At the peak of her ride, she didn't dampen her voice or squeeze her eyes shut but flashed them wide, and saw Phil Berg standing in the doorway back-lit by the hall's naked bulb, looking not at what she and his best friend were doing with his friend's hands cupped on her bare bottom, but he was looking straight into her eyes, marveling at her face of open surrender.

For days and weeks Rosemary couldn't separate what she had felt that night with her lover from what she felt with Phil Berg looking at her. And Phil could not shake his first impression of this woman: unguarded, and at her most vulnerable.

How do I know this? I don't. But it could have happened this way as well as any other. The more I think about it, it has to have happened this way. I'm trying to imagine what Rosemary might have lost when Phil walked out of her life, that would make her turn to someone so dead wrong as Buck, that would have made her choose Phil in the first place, what could possibly have happened in their first meeting that within the week she had left her fiancé and refused for months to speak to either man, and in fact didn't date again until spring, when one day, in midsentence, she felt this burning at the back of her neck and had an unaccountable urge to turn her head, and found Phil Berg staring at her, but only at her eyes, before he walked over to where she was standing, with books in arms, with half a dozen other young women with books in arms and sweaters draped around their shoulders, and, without a word, took her by the elbow and cut her apart from the pack.

They didn't get ten steps before Phil stopped and kissed her, pelvis to pelvis on the first kiss. None of the women doubted what would happen over the next few months, and none of the men felt they were ready to take on that kind of risk. They knew where that kind of love led—it led straight to disaster.

Stan says, "They were right, those friends of Phil's. People shouldn't feel things too deeply."

He's restringing the sash for Ted upstairs, and I can hardly breathe.

"You," he says, looking down at me through the window, "you're too sensitive. It'll make you crazy."

I'm halfway there, Stan. I can see the far shore.

Risk. Responsibility.

I left that job with the insurance agency not because I graduated, but because insurance presumes to equate a dollar value with a perceived risk. There is even a provision for acts of God, known in the trade as comprehensive. A hot-shot agent in the office had asked me to lunch one day and his hands were sweating. I told him,

Relax, I wasn't that hungry. He pulled up to a restaurant doing just fine, one I admired for its refusal to serve such green carnations as chop suey. The agent double-parked and handed me this envelope, a check with five zeros. "Give this to Mrs. Bertram Mak. Only to Mrs. Mak." He reached past me to open the door but ne-glected to tell me that her husband had been struck down at a controlled intersection—a clear day, a mas-sive bleed in the brain, peak physical condition for a man in his forties, a hospital two blocks away, and still he died. I had never seen a thirty-eight-year-old widow. Mrs. Mak stared at the envelope. I quit the next day. When God put up hurdles, did he imagine that we would try to lower the standards—with insurance?

Risk. When I'm peeved, I swim without a guard. I drive as fast as I can in dense fog. I stop in the park on the hill that links Rosemary's Orinda to my Berkeley—the park that Stan makes me swear never to drive in past ten at night. ("Bodies have been known to be dumped, why make yourself part of a lurid statistic?" Stan windsurfs, he hang-glides, he races dirt bikes and motorcycles. He has no problem with his own risk tak-ing, only with mine.) I stop in the park. I stop and I don't tell Stan. I love the thrill of being scared, a little more alive—but only when I'm vexed. I don't think about anyone else getting in my way. It's just selfish, ar-rogant me, my car, my matching the rhythm of the road just as fast as I dare. On a straight stretch I even close my eyes. All I'm risking is my life, which Mrs. Mak discovered the hard way has an immeasurable value. But, what was Rosemary Berg risking when she took Buck into her arms? Could she have been insured against that risk? And could that risk have been zoned and quantified and rated?

Stan gets up and covers my shoulders, not without great tenderness, but already he is somewhere else, as if what we had just achieved together has already become foam. Yet, this is how it must be, if we are to come together again with any fervor. This is the physics of love. Even tsunamis that have traveled thousands of miles will eventually flatten and dissipate into froth. Men understand this. They are made for this, moving on. But we are made differently from men. We receive into our bodies, their bodies, their secretions, their greatest gift. We have to stick around. In us is that dark and moist place of accommodation where cells thrive and divide and multiply.

I hunt him down on the job site, a massive basement conversion: game room/in-law/full bath/garden entry. "Stan," I say, and I whip him around.

"I need to go away, Stan, with you. To some untamable place with ferns that uncurl up to our eyeballs and still have a couple of feet's growth to go, and water that pours down the mountain in pool after pool after pool. Stan, now. I need to go *now*."

Stan holsters his hammer and leads me aside. Behind him the owner gets up from her home office computer to investigate the change in ambient noise. Any moment now I'm sure he'll say, *Did you take your vitamins today? Should I cook you liver for dinner?* But he doesn't. Instead he holds me tight. It hurts. On the ledge behind him is his carpenter's level, a behemoth three feet long. The bubble never lies.

A barometric disposition. Rosemary had it, and I think it's a contagion, this constant and uncontrollable urge for warring with, and flight from, the one you love. A sexual insatiability, an unabating heat and sweat, the beginning of the end of opportunity, of being filled with child, of being transported by this singular wonder. I think I want this. I want this. Big, big eyes fighting to stay awake as the child begs for his favorite story, a story he knows by heart and savors for its familiar turns, its predictable outcomes. Now he can sleep. He burrows in your side a mere kiss away, sees the book, smells the glue, but knows only that the story comes from you.

Prisoners are primed to confess the most absurd fictions (someone else's) after being denied sleep, this elegant torture that is admired for leaving no marks on the body. Senses dull. Irritability skyrockets. Judgments waver. Oh, sleep—deep, uninterrupted, mindless, dream sleep—whose visitations make it possible and clear just how one should begin a new day. Morpheus, you fickle lover. Tease. Where the hell are you? Five years without sleep, the doctors say, and you die.

"It's late," Stan gentles.

But I'm on a roll. I want to get it right. I forge, I anneal. Silver is harder than gold, but easier to work. Coat it on a sheet of glass, and it mirrors your very heart.

"You know, your rings will outlast the love. People change their minds. They die. Permanence is, at best, a good intention."

Dust smarts my eyes.

"Then there's no point in getting married."

"The point is, we still have to try. That's the point."

My man likes a challenge. He likes knocking down walls, seeing what problems lie within. A bath in the space of a closet? Stan installs the pedestal sink with the most generous lip and the smallest footprint; he recesses cabinets; mounts a mirror to open up the room; a skylight to give it lift. In the face of limitations, challenge becomes its own reward.

I sweep the ring graveyard, tossing into the garbage months of scraps and misses.

One beautiful thing. Before I die, I want to make just one beautiful, exquisite, durable thing.

No. Not rings.

Thick bands around wrists is where I'm headed.

Metal on metal. Metal peened and etched and fused. Something substantial, something with heft.

Over the months the cuffs gain in width, take on thickness and a veritable density, assume ever more fantastic proportions.

But—who will buy these pieces?

During the day, out on the street, I am the assembly line of every step that can be done without electricity: filing silver, cutting flat bands, shaping them into rings. These pieces are so straightforward they appeal, in every season, every year. I file, I schmooze ("Cleopatra wore lapis"), I sell as much as I can, and bargain when short. But at home, at night, I set aside all thoughts of commerce and work in earnest.

Stan brings a roast pork cilantro sandwich and gives me half in exchange for a stroll around the shop. His survey is thoughtful, is slow. So slow, I think I'm making a horrible mistake.

"Why silver, when we can afford gold?"

He's thinking about the effort for what many consider an inferior metal. Silver is less rare than gold, but does that make it inferior?

"Why silver? Why a sonata instead of a symphony? Why a bike instead of a motorcycle? Why remodel, Stan, when you can build brand-new on virgin plots?"

He picks up a piece I've copied from the Celts, is surprised by its lack of weight. A bar of cruciform twisted to a spiral—what looks solid is hollow. All those involuted curves, all that surface.

"It tarnishes."

"It's alive."

"It's unstable. Reactive."

"But, I don't mind that about silver."

Stan musses his own hair.

He has this walk—unconscious and fluid. He uses his body as one more tool in his box: fulcrum, buttress, mandrel to my ring. "Shape me," I say, but he has gone.

After weeks of lying in the dark, waiting for respite, listening to Stan sleep and being no more restored by listening than the homeless are warmed by looking into firelit rooms—it comes to me. A deep silver cuff, layers and layers of silver, a marriage of the rough and polished, and set not just with one stone, but *stones*. Brilliant, translucent, refractive stones—verdelite, alexandrite, emerald—all the colors of the green, green sea.

Clear stones don't sell on the street.

Faceted stones don't sell on the street.

And who can afford more than one, in the size I'm dreaming of? Yet these are the stones that I wake to. Dead of night I make sketches, reams of them.

The stones I acquire a few at a time, and to guard against discovery, I hide them in full view. At night, while Stan greases gears, I unfold white paper packets and spill colored prisms onto the bed: verdelites, peridots, aquamarines, emeralds, heliodors, blue topaz. Yesterday brought a packet of peridot pyramids in greens from lemon lime to olive. I can't tell if I'm more soothed by their color or by the beauty of equilateral triangles.

A hammered cuff, a cross of stones: four faceted peridots; and at the intersection, an oval chrysoprase. Would Stan wear this?

Silver—grooved and blackened—studded with alexandrites, stones that are green by day, red violet by night. Would Stan wear this?

Chased silver. A round of chrysoprase, a pyramid of onyx, a faceted garnet—opaques in green, black, and the bloody red. Would Stan wear this?

I arrange the cuffs in an old oak case. Suki walks over to see what I could be locking up under glass. Suki doesn't like green, she doesn't like clear stones, but she's all attention when I bring out the one with garnet, onyx, and chrysoprase. "I want that," she whispers. Accepting no argument and offering no money, she gives me instead a hand-colored print of waves—powerful, turbulent, golden waves—and we each tiptoe away feeling fortunate. All day Suki flashes that cuff. People *ooh* and *ahh*. A bold few ask to try on every new thing in the case, and in the end they buy what they've always come to the avenue to buy.

I set the best of the pieces on the ledge above the kitchen sink. Stan runs the tap and drinks his fill, sawdust in his hair. A passing kiss on the forehead. "Interesting," he says.

For the better part of a week I don't work. Instead I shop. I make soup, I read, I swim, sometimes twice in the same day, hoping to barter fatigue for a couple more hours of sleep.

The stones are wrong, I see that now. Green is my color, not Stan's. Green water is river water, pond water. And while there are pristine pockets all over the world where even the sea is green, when one thinks of big water, one sees blue. Blue is what Stan reaches for when he finds the stones on the bed. He lies alongside me and plucks out from among the swirling green stones the single sapphire.

"Did Stevie B really go through the windshield and land on the freeway?"

I nod.

"Did he—die?"

For years I'd wake to the sounds of his moaning. "It might have been kinder if he had."

Stan's lips brush my shoulder. How could anything manly be so soft?

After a while he takes my hand and lays the sapphire in the valley between two fingers.

The court stones—sapphires, emeralds—are cut into lavish teardrops and octagons, set in platinum, and pressed all around by diamonds like the honor elite guarding the queen of the free world—and if anything could be called dazzling, these jewels are it. Indeed the combination nearly screams, this extrovert jewelry, once the reserve of kings and queens and popes. How can anyone sleep with such brilliance on their bodies?

Substituting silver for platinum seems nothing short of willful. But I won't work with gold, some genetic defect. Platinum-silver/silver-platinum. I seesaw for days.

Paper-thin sheets, ten, twenty sheets of silver (OK, some gold, too) sandwiched into a Dagwood of a cuff. I solder the edges together. The edges don't quite line up, the gold peeks through. I make more slashes. The gold swells. Stones ride the wavy surface.

I step back, walk around the piece. Leave it. Come back. Have lunch. Bring it out in the sun, under the moon. Walk around it some more.

Silver. Platinum. Platinum. Silver.

Silver.

Honest, everyday silver. It has to be silver.

Sapphires and silver.

I'm committing lapidary sacrilege, I know. But making this promise to sapphire and silver, I'm all patience now. But blue—I can't get excited about blue. Except maybe with black. Blue and black. Sapphires and onyx. No. Oh, no.

Dusk.

Winter near, the crisp air nips the skin. When the air

is forty degrees, the water seems downright amniotic. I'm in the water so long, I've lost track of time. Other swimmers come and go, come and go. The one-mile mark looms and it's a smooth, at-ease swim. Loose, I'm so loose, just another lap, another and another—in a rhythm true enough to set clocks, to beat out a song, to slip all the way through the night—until I find myself at foreign shores, approaching twenty-five hundred yards (don't stop, don't even think about it), twenty-seven hundred, three thousand yards. And at that distance—what's another six hundred?

An hour and a half. Two miles out.

No bells go off, no one cheers, but the stars have come out and I've tasted that sweet pace at which a person could just keep going, all day long, all night. Two miles!

I roll over on my back and drift, not yet feeling the aches that will surely follow. Marley, the guard, grins from her perch. "You're ready," she says. And for a moment I believe her. I contemplate taking on the beast of my dreams—the open-water swim.

It is in this natatory trance that I see the piece in its entirety: a silver cuff, yes. A deep silver cuff, layers of silver. Sapphires—yes. Oh, yes. But no onyx.

I throw wet gear into my bag and sprint home. So obvious, right in front of me, all along.

Silver loves to be black.

The finish has to be black. Acetylene black, the blackest black.

A cowboy, with hand-tooled red-and-black boots that looked like he had had for maybe thirty years and loved them every minute, stops at my table, looks everything over in a glance, and asks don't I have something else to show him. When I don't answer right away he looks up. One of his eyes is lazy and does not track. The black cuff, the new black cuff, the black cuff so new neither Stan nor Suki has seen it, is wrapped in a piece of velvet, tucked inside my canvas bag. I toe the bag a little farther under the table and draw the man's attention to some turquoise I'm sure he's seen the Navajos do better and cheaper. He sucks the air through his teeth. "Are you *sure* there's nothing else?" Suki stops in midsentence. The cuff glows. It's damn near radioactive. Some somnambulistic me pulls out the velvet, unfolds the cloth. *No, don't!* There it is: a black cuff of sterling, splashed with sapphires, streamed with gold, and washed with pinpoint diamonds. The cowboy stares at it, then brings the cuff up to his good eye. A desperate, muttering man bursts out of the rooming hotel with diapered son in tow, curses his haggard wife, and slaps his daughter when she begins to sing. Suki reaches for her baseball bat. The cowboy holds the cuff between us

and says, "The sea. At night." Neither of us breathes. It
is all I can do to keep from snatching the cuff from him.
Instead, I name some obscene price. The cowboy grins,
lays down cash money in an inch-thick wad of fifties,
takes possession, and steps back into the shade.

I've been sitting out on the back porch for an hour,
maybe two. People finish late and staggered dinners,
they brush their teeth at the kitchen sink, and down-
load their days to anyone who will half listen. Shirts
come off, robes on. Hair is released from clips and combs
and elastic bands, bare feet are propped up on kitchen
chairs while arms are crossed over unbound breasts—
and one is not even aware of one's own contradictory
messages. At some point people just stop talking to
each other and rush to their own respective needs, often
while still in the same room. They tidy their lives in an
uncontemplative and tooled bliss. I wonder how I can
get some of that. I wonder, once having gotten it, would
I then be able to sleep?

Midnight. The Y just locked its doors; the Plunge
won't open for another six hours. I'm longing for a
swim, to be immersed in water, to be in its surround,
floating, drifting, lost—in water. It wouldn't take much
to get in the car and drive to Stinson Beach, an hour,
less. Just slip into the Pacific. Silver can be found in
seawater, in trace amounts.

The red giant blinks, a star in its last hours of burning, the one pink sapphire in Orion's belt. Stan is right. Nothing is perfect, nothing is forever, not gold, not silver, not diamonds, not even the stars in their brilliant, sustained death.

Something will happen in one of these yards: murmuring voices, unbridled laughter—sounds that always seem more sterling coming from someone else's mouth. Not isolated events, but an infectious rippling, a compelling current strong enough to carry along even me.

Out of nowhere, Stan. I don't hear him so much as smell the sum of his labors and consumption embedded on his shirt, on his skin, in the oils of his hair. He comes to me and I cushion him. The sky opens wide between the rooftops and we reclaim our humility in all that possibility. We are out there for some time and I think about going in, but Stan says, "Stay with me, Ruby." He laces his fingers deeply into mine and stretches my webs with his girth, and I feel real heat between my legs. Does he also say, *Don't be afraid*? And even though I've been waiting all these years for a hint of the engagement we once had, I'm still swept along by the depth of his color, by his translucence, by the fullness of his face as he becomes an even more vivid version of himself— as if some god has taken over his shape, and infused him with the very energy that makes life. Everything is a swirl, is a struggle—to be with him, to get away—and it is all I can do to ignore the sand already giving way under my feet and meet him with everything I have. Anyone happening down the stairs with the garbage can glimpse our tandem motion, can hear our accelerating rhythm, our every desperate declaration—which I now hear so well are simply fervent pleas for grace.

A number of people gave generously of their time and expertise: jewelers Katherine Brewer and Diana Yoshida explained their craft and tools, corrected drafts, and contributed a rich, lapidary vernacular; Raymond Louis, David Louis, M.D., and Warren Nelson, M.D., answered legal and medical queries; Joanne Jauregui supplied the deaf tree joke and the story of the origin of sign language used in "Talking in the Dark"; David Corbett, Amy Gottlieb, Arlene Sagan, Edith Kasin, and Ruth Reynolds all braved stories in early drafts. I borrowed liberally from designs and techniques of Yasuki Hiramatsu and Barbara Tipple in imagining the bracelet Ruby might make in "Divining the Waters." Finally, I owe a debt to the reference librarians at the Berkeley Public Library, who take calls an amazing seven days a week. I thank these fine people and beg forgiveness for anything I may have failed to understand, and of anyone I may have forgotten.

About the Cantonese: unlike Mandarin, there is no standard for the Romanization of the Cantonese dialect. I consulted Parker Po-Fei Huang's *Cantonese Dictionary* (Yale University Press, 1970).